AN

## Arcadia Valley

### ROMANCE

www.ArcadiaValleyRomance.com

# Secrets of the Heart

Arcadia Valley Series
Book 1

# LEE TOBIN McCLAIN

# CHAPTER ONE

JAVIER QUINTANA RAKED his fingers through his hair and tried to concentrate on the laptop in front of him and the stack of bills beside him. The empty dining room of El Corazon provided no distraction.

The restaurant wasn't going under...at least not yet. But it was definitely in the red.

He looked up at the portrait of his mother and father on the wall. They'd started El Corazon as newlyweds. All four of the kids had grown up there, hanging around, helping, doing homework at this very table, moving back into the kitchen when the dinner rush started.

Now, there wasn't much of a dinner rush.

He'd promised his father, and then his mother, to keep the restaurant in the family and to keep it going.

The cold, dry bills and papers around him seemed to crush the colorful, happy place his parents had made.

Behind him, the restaurant's front door opened.

"We're closed," he called without looking up.

"Hello?" The voice sounded like... No, it couldn't be. He straightened his shirt as he strode through the entryway to the door.

And froze.

Molly?

In a flash he was eighteen again, in love with his whole young heart.

He blinked and refocused his eyes. Yes, Molly Abbot stood there, framed by the golden light of a late-August day.

His heart stopped, stuttered, and then settled into pounding, hard and fast.

She was even more beautiful than she'd been in high school. Big eyes, cornsilk blonde hair full around her shoulders. She was still a tiny little thing, dressed professionally now, but with the big, dangly earrings she'd always favored.

Yes, it was the same Molly he'd loved.

The same Molly who'd betrayed him.

Anger drew him up to his full six-two, and it was only his wired-in manners that prevented him from slamming the door in her face, shutting out the beauty and the pain.

"Hey, Javier, it's definitely been awhile." She seemed to be looking past him into the restaurant.

He crossed his arms and clenched his jaw.

"I was supposed to meet you guys here... Veronica said you knew all about it. Maybe I'm a little early?"

She checked her watch. "I can come back when everyone's here. I don't want to be a way from my daughter too long—"

What meeting was she talking about? And how could she have the audacity to talk to him about her daughter?

He tried to school his face, to focus on the chirping birds and crickets, the hot air pushing its way through the open door behind her and into the restaurant's air-conditioned coolness. From the parking lot, the sweet aroma of pineapple weed blew in.

"Or, maybe this is a blessing." Her hand came up to twist her hair. "Maybe we can talk a little."

He still hadn't said one word to her and she seemed to realize that, finally. She looked down at the ground, or maybe she was just checking out the way the parking lot's dust had taken the shine off her designer shoes.

"Can I come in?"

No.

No way.

He stepped back to let her pass. Why was she here? Why, after all this time, and acting like she belonged here?

She walked in and did a turn around the dining room, totally calm. Analytical, almost. "The place still looks the same."

Love and pain surged up at her words, covered

over with a glaze of terrible, terrible hurt.

This was nothing to her. She felt nothing.

He swallowed down his emotions, trying to make way for some civilized words to pass, but he couldn't quite get there. "Don't try to make small talk." He knew his voice was harsh. "You're not welcome."

She looked at him full on then, met his eyes with her blue ones. She didn't look ashamed. More like surprised, and maybe a little angry.

Car doors slammed in the parking lot, and a few seconds later his brothers and sister pushed into the restaurant. "Hey, Javier! We're here!"

"Molly beat us." Veronica reached out and hugged Molly, which felt to Javier like a betrayal. "Hey, girl, how are you?"

"Sorry we're late, we would've been on time if it weren't for lover boy here." Daniel punched Alex in the arm.

Alex held his hands up like stop signs. "Hey, I had to help my girl move into her new apartment. What else does a fiancé do?" He seemed to be trying to keep a silly grin off his face, but it wasn't working.

A slight feeling of satisfaction pushed past Javier's distress. It was good to see Alex so happy. One of his siblings had found a good woman, at least.

They'd come to a stop in a semicircle around him, all quieting down a little. Javier was the oldest brother, and since Papa had died, he'd been the head of the family. They treated him with respect rather than the clowning around they did with each other. But right now, his brothers and his sister had identical guilty looks in their eyes.

He couldn't bear to look at Molly, to try to dissect whatever she might be feeling.

He cleared his throat. "What memo did I miss?"

Veronica stepped forward and put an arm around him, leaning her head against his shoulder. "We're kind of doing an intervention."

"We know how hard you've been working," Alex began, and then broke off. Despite having been a big-deal major league baseball player, he tended to defer to his older brothers.

"And we know the restaurant isn't doing real well." Daniel perched on the edge of a table, looking around the room. Whatever they were up to must be serious, to get Daniel to actually come to the restaurant.

"I want to help, but once I start school and this new job, I won't have much time," Alex said.

Daniel twisted his head from side to side and pushed clasped hands out in front of him, stretching his neck. Chiropracting on himself. "I have no life as it is, what with the girls and my practice. You already know I'm no use to you."

"And even though I'm here every day, I can't figure out how to fix whatever's wrong with El

Corazon," Veronica said. "Plus, you turned down the other two consultants we brought in…"

It was true. He had. They'd been idiots. "Get to the point."

"We kind of decided something on our own," Veronica said.

"Took it to a vote," Alex said, "and all three of us agreed, so… "

"We went ahead and hired Molly." Daniel said, his voice firm. He put an arm around Molly's shoulders.

A flush of angry heat rose in Javier's face and neck, whether because of the idea that they'd hired her, or because of Daniel touching her, he couldn't say for sure.

"She's a food entrepreneur," Veronica explained, "who knows all about the fresh-food movement."

"She turned around three restaurants in Cleveland."

"One of them's a traditional Mexican place."

"And she knows El Corazon, because she practically spent high school here."

Which was exactly the problem. She'd humiliated him in front of the entire town.

She shrugged out from under Daniel's arm and held up a slender, delicate hand, looking from Javier to Veronica, Daniel, and Alex. "Hold up. I thought Javier knew about this and agreed to it."

His siblings all started to talk, but she put a hand on her hip and shook her head. "From the preliminary research I've done, he's the main manager and the rest of you are only peripherally involved, Daniel not at all." She frowned severely at them. "And you sprung this on him?"

"You know how he is, Mol." Alex lifted his hands, palms up.

"Stubborn and bull-headed," Veronica added.

He was watching her—he couldn't help it—so he saw the emotion that flashed across her face. She did know how he was.

Something else flashed: the small silver cross around her neck, the same one she'd worn back when he'd known her in high school. He remembered touching it when he'd kissed her. It had reminded him of her purity and kept him from going too far.

She hadn't held to the same rules with the next guy, obviously.

"I want her out of here."

She raised her eyebrows and looked at him steadily for a few seconds, then looked around at his siblings. "So, I'm going to go back to Uncle Dale's house and help my daughter get ready for the first day of school." She paused, and then spoke again. "We do have a back-out clause in the contract, but I hope it won't come to that since I've pulled up stakes and moved." She gave Javier a cool glance. And then, her back straight, she stalked out of the restaurant.

Immediately, his brothers and sister started talking.

"That was so rude!" Veronica slapped his arm.

"No way to talk to a lady," Alex scolded.

"We can't afford her back-out clause." That was Daniel, his worry lines—perpetual with him since the loss of his wife—deepening in his face. "If we don't hire her, I don't know what else we can do."

"Just because you never got over her..."

He held up a hand. "Stop."

"But—"

"I mean it. Stop."

They all shut their mouths, thankfully, though he knew that wouldn't last.

"I don't appreciate your doing this without consulting me. You know, just like everyone else in town, what happened between us thirteen years ago. Why would you think we could work together?"

"But would you have hired her if you'd known?" Veronica asked.

"I'm telling you, she's the only person who can do this for us," Alex said. "She knows the fresh-food culture, and she knows our traditions."

"You have issues," Daniel said. "You don't trust women."

"You should talk," Veronica said, elbowing Daniel.

"I don't trust *her*," Javier said flatly.

"See, this is your problem." Veronica pushed herself into the curve of his arm. As the little sister, she could get away with saying things their brothers couldn't, and she knew it. "You have to do everything yourself, you're over-responsible, you're controlling. Right now, that's not working."

"Look," Alex said, "we all want the best for El Corazon. We hate to see it go under. But when you were in Mexico and I was running the place, I saw the truth. That's where we're heading."

"I'm just not ready for that." Veronica's voice sounded shaky. "I'm not ready to lose this world I grew up in. The world Mama and Papa made." She glanced over at the portrait of their parents.

Javier looked at it, too, and then stared down at the tile floor. As the oldest brother, it was his job to care for them. Right now, he was more of an impediment to getting things done, at least from the way they were describing it.

Not only that, he was outnumbered. They all four had a quarter interest in the restaurant, and if three of them had made a decision, he should—had to, really— go along with it.

But work with Molly Abbot? The woman who'd played him for a fool and broken his heart?

"I'll think about it," he growled just to get them out of his hair. "Now, everybody needs to leave. I've got work to do."

*FOCUS ON RIGHT now,* Molly told herself after a dinner she'd cooked but hadn't been able to eat. A walk, fresh air, and a little back-to-school shopping with Trina would settle her nerves. And although Uncle Dale had been nothing but kind about letting them stay with him for a bit, he wasn't well, and he wasn't used to a twelve-year-old's moods and loud music. He needed a little time to himself.

"It's so cute!" Trina sped up as Arcadia Valley's tree-lined Main Street came into view. "Come on, Mom!"

"I'm coming." Molly walked more slowly, taking in the sights and sounds of her small hometown after twelve years away. Arcadia Valley held wonderful memories for Molly, but they were overshadowed by the horrific last thing that happened to her here.

Now that she was raising an almost-teenager, though, the good outweighed the bad. Trina needed a place like Arcadia Valley. And for her daughter's sake, she was willing to face her demons.

If, that is, Javier Quintana let her keep the job she'd been promised.

"I wonder if girls dress up for the first day of school here like they did in Cleveland." Trina hopped along beside Molly now, holding onto her arm like a little kid. That was a twelve-year old: clinging one moment, pushing Mom away the next.

"What to wear might not be as important here as it was in the city," Molly said, hoping it was true.

"Mom, it's always important. Look at that girl. She's wearing patterned leggings, and I only have black ones. Can we go shopping for more school clothes after this?"

"Not tonight," Molly said automatically. "We have to budget for new things." They did okay, her work brought in good money, but she was the sole support of herself and Trina. After the school shopping they'd already done, she had fifty dollars left in their clothing budget for August.

Trina's lower lip stuck out. "I bet *she* doesn't have to budget. Her whole outfit is cute and it's not even school yet."

Molly looked ahead at the girl her daughter was watching and her heart almost stopped. The girl and another teen were walking with someone who looked an awful lot like Javier Quintana.

It couldn't be, could it? There were lots of tall, dark-haired men in this part of the country.

The man turned a little to the side to talk to one of the girls, and all doubt left Molly's mind. It was Javier.

"Let's get ice cream!" She tugged Trina toward a small café with a sign advertising fifteen flavors. "In here."

"I'm not that hungry. If we have ice cream, we

won't be able to go into the shoe place. Let's get it after."

Molly sighed. Her daughter was definitely becoming a teen, if she were more interested in shoes than ice cream. Now more than ever, Molly had to set a good example for her daughter and not be intimidated by a man.

When she glanced up the street, Molly saw that Javier and the girls had disappeared from sight. She breathed a little easier. She just wasn't ready to face Javier again, not until she'd figured out a plan to get him on her side.

There was the back-out clause in the contract, but she desperately wanted to raise Trina in Arcadia Valley. Desperately wanted to settle down now that Trina was twelve. Desperately wanted to help Uncle Dale, the man who'd provided warmth and comfort to her when she was prickly and miserable, grieving the loss of her parents.

She'd find a way to convince Javier to keep her on, but not tonight when her nerves were ragged and her stomach tense and jittery.

They continued down the street. Molly gave herself an inner pep talk while Trina chattered and tugged her arm to look in various shop windows.

Minutes later they reached their destination. "Look," Molly said, forcing cheer into her voice, "Wallman's Shoes. They've been here since I was a kid, and they're the best." Molly didn't add that when she was a teenager, her own shoes had come from the discount store. She was just glad she could provide better for her own daughter.

Inside, Trina headed automatically to the sale racks—Molly had trained her well—and after greeting the saleswoman, Molly followed her daughter. The store was hot and smelled of leather.

"I just wish I knew what kids wear here. I don't want to be the only dork in high tops if everyone else wears ankle boots."

"You don't have to be like everyone else." Molly picked up a pair of marked-down Sergio Rossi pumps in her own size, running a finger over the rich leather. *If only.* "You're an individual, and anyway, confidence is the most important thing."

"If I look different, they'll tease me." Trina said it matter-of-factly, the voice of experience.

For the millionth time, Molly bemoaned the affluent public school Trina had attended back in Cleveland, where clothes had been crucial and mean girls ruled the hallways. She'd thought she was doing the right thing, renting an inexpensive apartment in a fantastic school district, but once Trina's elementary school years were over, everything had gone downhill for her.

A low, rumbling voice on the other side of the sale rack played along Molly's nerves and made the hairs on the back of her neck stand up. A moment later, the two girls who'd been with Javier came around the edge of the sale rack. "We can show you what kids wear here," the older one said. "Come up front."

"Really?" In Trina's face, mistrust battled the desire to make new friends. She looked up at Molly.

With her mom-radar, Molly scanned the other girls' features and detected only a wary friendliness. "Are you Mr. Quintana's nieces?" she asked.

"Kind of," the younger girl said. "Our mom is his cousin, so I guess we're really... well, whatever. We call him Uncle Javier."

"Can I, Mom?"

"Go ahead. I'll be here."

Trina headed off with the other two girls, smiling shyly.

Molly stood frozen, her heart pounding.

"I was rude to you today." Javier came around the edge of the shoe rack. "I apologize." His voice was toneless.

When Molly looked up at him, memories and emotions flooded her. She looked at the rack of shoes, focusing on the practical canvas ones she ought to buy herself next month. "It's not that so much. I've been in business awhile, I know clients can be emotional about changes. It's just that... I moved us here hoping this job would make for a smooth transition. Financially, I mean. So your resistance is a little worrisome." She hazarded a glance at Javier's arm and noticed he had a tattoo. It reminded her that he'd been in the service since they'd known each other. He had a whole life, probably including a wife or a girlfriend.

"I promised my brothers and sister I'd think about hiring you." He picked up a pair of spike-heeled pumps, shook his head, and put them back.

How long would his thinking process take?

The truth was, Javier had pushed her away at the most painful time of her life, and she still carried anger and hurt from that.

Of course, he hadn't known the whole story, and she hadn't told him.

She glanced up and then quickly looked away. Javier was still so handsome it squeezed her chest tight.

Sweat trickled down her sides. Man, was it hot in here.

The girls were giggling over by the shoe displays. One of them had a phone, and as Molly watched, she snapped selfies of the three of them, holding up various shoes. Trina struck a silly pose and the others laughed.

Relief washed over Molly, even in her exhaustion and tension. It was good to see Trina making friends, good to see kids just being kids.

She looked up to see Javier smiling over at the girls, too. So he wasn't stone-faced all of the time.

He still had a killer smile.

Trina saw them watching and came rushing over, banging into Molly with a hard hug, all elbows and knees. "Mom! Laura and Raquel say a lot of the girls wear boots like this the first day." She thrust a pair of fleece-lined suede boots at Molly. "Can I get these instead of shoes, please?"

Molly checked the price tag on the bottom of the boots. $110.00.

"Please, Mom? I know it's more than the budget but I'll... I'll help Uncle Dale in the yard, and do the dishes every night, and—"

"Wait." Molly used her phone to check her bank balance, conscious of Javier's eyes on her. An argument pounded her already aching head.

Aunt Lisa to a much younger Molly, when she'd begged for a sky-blue sweater in the style worn by the cool girls: "When you're earning your own money you can buy whatever clothes you want. Until then, Gambino's Discount is perfectly good."

The teacher from the money management class at church: "It's the little decisions you make that add up to never reaching your goals."

She didn't want to raise her daughter the cold way Aunt Lisa had raised her. She'd promised herself she'd be warm, loving, open.

But would a particular type of boots really help Trina to fit in at school? And what lesson did she want to teach her daughter about money?

The numbers swam a little before her eyes. She really should have eaten something at dinner. "No, honey. Choose a pair in our price range for now."

"Aw, Mom!" Trina looked at Molly as if to see if she meant it, and then stalked off.

Trina wasn't the only one upset; Javier was looking at her suspiciously. Was it because she wouldn't buy her daughter boots, or because he thought Trina was the product of an affair she'd had while dating him? She swayed a little and grabbed onto the shoe rack for support. The lack of food and sleep was catching up with her. "I'm going to sit down," she told Javier, and aimed at the row of chairs for shoe customers.

Halfway there, she felt Javier's firm hand under her elbow. He guided her to a seat and then knelt beside her, looking up at her face.

His touch, his closeness, brought back all sorts of feelings she shouldn't be having. She could smell his faint cologne, the same he'd used in high school.

She took deep breaths, trying to control her dizziness. Maybe he still cared about her. Or at least, maybe he didn't hate her.

"Are you okay?" he asked. "Don't tell me you're pregnant again?"

His words hit her like a blow.

"Sorry," he said with a nervous laugh. "Bad joke,

huh?"

She didn't answer his question, just called to Trina. "Come on, honey. It's time to go. Make your choice." She stood, and Javier did too, so she stepped away, taking deep breaths and straightening her spine. Good. She didn't feel dizzy anymore. Just angry.

"Hey, are you sure you're okay?" Javier asked.

Molly ignored him and walked over to where the girls were.

A few minutes later, Trina had chosen some shoes approved by the other two girls and within their budget, and Molly had paid for them. As they headed out the door, Trina stopped and turned back. "Bye, Raquel. Bye, Laura."

"It was nice to meet you," Laura said, and all three of them—the two girls and Javier—came across the store toward the door, too.

"We'll see you at school," Raquel said. "You'll like it here."

"I already like it," Trina said, and looked up at Molly. "Can we stay in Arcadia Valley, Mom?"

Molly looked down at her beloved daughter and brushed back her hair. "I hope so, honey." Or *did* she hope so? Could she subject herself to more insults from the only man she'd ever loved? "We'll have to see."

# CHAPTER TWO

JAVIER'S PALMS WERE sweating. No matter how many times you walked into a middle school, you never escaped that rush of memory. The sharp, half-pleasant smell of cleaning chemicals. Newly waxed floors and rows of lockers. Kids' voices, talking, joking, and yelling.

He'd volunteered to bring his nieces to the day-before-school-starts introductory event so he could find Molly and apologize for being a jerk. He still intended to boot her out of town, but he didn't want to do it on such a bad note. The image of her hurt eyes had haunted him last night.

Why had he blurted out such a dumb remark? Who asked a woman if she were pregnant?

"Oh no." Next to him, his niece Laura nudged her sister. "Mean Team Number One has found Trina."

Javier looked in the direction Laura indicated and saw Trina close to her mother's side. Molly wore a slim-fitting pink dress and sandals, and she outshone all the other moms like a princess among the peasants.

At least to him.

He clenched his jaw, forced his eyes away from Molly, and scanned the area surrounding the pair. "Who's the mean team?"

"The tall one in the green shirt and jeans, with her two friends. They're whispering and laughing."

That described about every cluster of girls near Molly and Trina, but then he saw three of the girls look pointedly at Trina and then confer together, laughing. Molly put an arm around Trina, and Trina said something sharp and shook it off, her expression miserable.

"I can't stand them." Raquel waved to Trina.

"Stop it." Laura grabbed her sister's arm. "They'll start picking on us."

"I'm not afraid of Xenia Smith and her sidekicks. Hey, Trina!" She waved bigger.

Trina saw the girls and her face broke into a relieved smile. Without a backward glance at Molly, she rushed toward her new friend.

Molly started to follow, but a male teacher who'd been shepherding kids toward the auditorium touched her arm and spoke to her. She smiled and said something, and the two of them shook hands.

At which point Javier recognized Mike Milosovich, who attended Javier's church and who seemed to have a knack for befriending pretty, single women.

It had never bothered Javier before.

Mike must have made some kind of a joke, because Molly laughed. The familiar, husky sound of it crossed the thinning crowd of kids to dance along Javier's nerve endings.

"We're going into the auditorium, Uncle Javier." Laura was tugging at his sleeve as if she'd said the same thing several times.

"Oh, sure. That's fine. I'll be here."

"There's a parents' part you're supposed to go to, in half an hour," Raquel informed him as if he should have known it. Probably, he should have. His attention had been elsewhere.

He refocused on his nieces and Trina, watching as they moved toward the auditorium, following the instructions of several harassed-looking teachers. Then he turned back to find Molly at his side.

"You sure spend a lot of time with your cousin's daughters." She looked curious. Skeptical.

"You think I'm stalking you?" He meant the remark to sound humorous, but it came out as a genuine question. In fact, he *had* come to this event in the hopes of seeing her. To make one apology. That was the only reason.

She didn't need *him* to stalk her. Mike Milosovich could do a fine job of that.

"Their mom just had surgery," he explained quickly. "She's alone, so I help out days when I can, since my work's more at night." He cleared his throat. "I also hoped to see you and apologize."

She crossed her arms and looked up at him, not speaking.

"I'm sorry I made that comment last night. It was rude and intrusive, and I shouldn't have said it." There. Now to get on with getting rid of her, because looking into her eyes like this was intense.

"Thanks." She didn't say he was forgiven.

He looked away to regroup and noticed a boy and girl hanging back from going into the auditorium. The boy, tall and lanky and acne-faced, was wiping his hands along the side of his jeans. The girl looked cool and calm.

He flashed back to high school days of trying to talk to Molly, to get up the nerve to ask her out. What a triumph it had been when she'd finally said yes, and how much like a man he'd felt with her on his arm.

Look how *that* had turned out.

Clusters of parents remained outside the auditorium, talking, and he noticed a couple of women looking their way with nosy curiosity on their faces. A chubby blonde woman detached herself from the small crowd and started to walk briskly toward them.

Escape time. "Listen, can we talk a few minutes before the parents' part of the program? About the restaurant." No need to give her the idea he wanted to be personal.

"Where?"

"There are some benches outside the office." He shepherded her that way, touching the small of her back and then yanking his hand back before it could settle there.

"Look," he said as they walked, "I'm sorry my family asked you to come work for us. It's their mistake. They shouldn't have hired you."

"According to them, it's needed to save your restaurant from going under."

"They exaggerate."

"I need this job for my daughter. And for Uncle Dale."

He let himself be distracted by the thought of Molly's large, jovial uncle, who'd seemed happy to take Molly in when she'd been a young teenager. "What's going on with him? Are you staying there?"

"He's had some health problems and he's not taking care of himself. So we're staying for a few weeks, until we can get the lay of the land and find our own place. Preferably not too far, so we can keep helping him with doctor appointments and such."

"Where's your aunt?" He could already guess the answer.

"She's abroad. I guess Paris is lovely in autumn. But let's talk about the job."

"Fair enough. Do you want to sit down?" He gestured toward a bench.

She sat and then he did, a good few feet away.

"Let me tell you how I usually work," she said. "I like to observe as a customer a few times, some with management there and some without. Then I make a recommendation or a series of them, we decide on a plan together, and I offer as much help as needed to implement—"

"I researched your work and—"

"Let me finish?"

"Sorry." He couldn't quite believe this poised, polished professional was the insecure Molly Abbott he'd known in high school.

"Your siblings would like me to stay and help you implement the plan. So there's a financial incentive to do that written into the contract."

Heat rose up Javier's neck as the sense of being railroaded into something nudged at his pride. "I don't understand why you moved here for one job."

She drew in a long, slow breath and let it out, shaking her head.

"You don't think it's my business. It's not for a client to know. But that's just it, Molly. I'm more than a client because we have a history."

She held up a hand like she didn't want him to go into it. "I get it. You're right, I guess." She frowned. "That's just how Trina and I have lived. We've moved three times during her school years alone. But with her getting older, I've started developing the online side of my business, and it should be up and running in a few months." She went on, explaining her business and her plans.

Javier had a hard time paying attention to the details. He couldn't stop focusing on how pretty she was. That, in turn, made him annoyed with himself.

"I'd have to travel a little, even if the business were mostly online," she said, "but Uncle Dale and Aunt Lisa could help with Trina at those times. And there are a lot of other restaurants in this region, so if I do well at El Corazon, I know I can get more projects. This part of the country is ripe for green remakes."

She sounded confident and professional, and having researched her business online, he knew she had an excellent track record.

And she drew him in in ways he barely understood. He only knew that it was dangerous. "What will you do if I don't agree?"

Her forehead wrinkled. "I guess... I'll have to look for other clients around here. It would be better if I had a local success under my belt, but..." She shrugged. "I'll try to make it work. I have to."

"You're committed to staying in this area? Why?"

She scooted a little away from him and leaned back against the wall. "Trina has had some trouble. She's a little young for her age, and in middle school, girls can be awful to each other. She... got into some trouble last year because of associating with some older kids who weren't a great influence. Speaking of which…" She put a hand on his arm and the warmth of it travelled instantly to his heart. "I really appreciate your nieces being so nice to her. That's exactly what she needs."

"They were brought up to be kind. We all were."

"I know, Javier. I remember."

Her quiet words brought back the memory of a group of girls teasing Molly about something, he didn't even know what. His sister Veronica, much younger, had been playing at the park, seen what was happening, and run to get Javier. He'd walked in and made them stop, Veronica a tiny spitfire beside him.

That might have been his first interaction with Molly, outside of school.

Their eyes met and held. Then she looked away. "Teasing can happen anywhere, but it was worse where we were living. Trina needs to be at a smaller school in a welcoming town like Arcadia Valley."

A forty-something woman whom Javier remembered as a neighbor of Molly's aunt and uncle approached. "Is that Molly Abbott?"

Molly stood. "Mrs. Johnson. How are you doing?"

"I'm well, thank you. Surprised to see you back in town, and to see you two together."

Molly looked puzzled, and then gave a barely visible shrug and turned the tables. "What brings you to the school? The twins must be off to college by now."

"They are. I'm an aide for one of the students."
She looked Molly up and down as if she were performing a style analysis.

"Well, it's nice to see you. Give my best to Mr. Johnson."

"Of course." The older woman strode off.

Molly looked after her, a puzzled expression on her face.

"She remembers your history here," he said by way of explanation. "Aren't you afraid other people will, too?"

She spun to face him, hands on hips. "Everyone isn't as old fashioned as you are! It's the twenty-first century and single mothers aren't outcasts!" She took a step back, her face flushed.

She glanced toward the hallway where the other parents were still audible, and fear flickered in her eyes.

So she wasn't as confident as she acted.

"It's a small town," he said, "and what happened was pretty public."

She lifted her chin. "You have no idea of what happened, and I don't want to discuss it."

Her inherent dignity pushed him back to a middle school mindset, where he didn't get any of the emotional nuances, only dimly knew he was misunderstanding something. "I'm sorry. You're right. Water under the bridge."

How did it happen that *he* was feeling guilty, when she was the one who'd betrayed him?

Sounds came from the auditorium, kids' voices, English and Spanish. Their gathering was breaking up, and the portion of the program for parents and guardians was coming next.

"We need this job, Javier."

He stood, looked at her seriously. She was holding herself together, but she was upset, he could tell. Unbidden, a verse from the Bible came to him, something about helping widows and orphans in their distress.

Why he'd think of that in connection with never-married Molly, and Trina who had a perfectly good and alive mother, at least, he didn't know.

"I'd like to get started. I'd like to visit El Corazon tonight during the dinner hour. I'll bring Uncle Dale and Trina and just get some impressions. What do you say?"

He scrubbed a hand over his face. "You're relentless, you know that?"

For the first time in their encounter, a smile tugged at the corner of her mouth. "Most of my clients consider that a plus. I can turn El Corazon around, Javier. I can help you make it thrive. Keep your parents' legacies alive."

He bit back the words he'd been about to say. Molly understood him. She knew that family and legacy were the most important things. "You know exactly how to get to me, don't you?"

She lifted an eyebrow. "I do know you pretty well. Or at least, I did at one time." A cloud passed over her face. "Of course, a lot has changed since then. Almost everything."

He shouldn't do it. He should stop this right here, because it wasn't going to work long term.

"We'll pay for our dinner, how about that?" She offered a tentative smile. "Are you in any position to turn away paying customers?"

He wasn't, of course. "The dinner will be on the house," he said with a sense of impending disaster, "and afterward, we'll talk. But I have to tell you, Molly. I don't think this is going to work."

MOLLY LED TRINA AND UNCLE DALE into El Corazon, trying to ignore the way her heart jumped at the possibility of seeing Javier. He'd been kind but edgy, obviously still hung up on what had happened years ago.

When actually, he didn't have a clue about the assault that had stolen her innocence and changed her world. And she had no intention of telling him.

"I always liked El Corazon," Uncle Dale said as Veronica Quintana greeted them and led them to a seat, giving Molly an encouraging squeeze of the arm.

"You don't hear too much about it now, but in its time it was one of the best restaurants in the valley."

Veronica winced as she handed out menus. "Ouch. The truth hurts. I'm hoping we'll go back to being just that, with Molly's help."

Molly focused on the details of the restaurant, filtering what she saw through her experience and schooling.

The dining room was half full, pretty good for a Tuesday. Until you factored in the other dining room that stood dark and empty. The décor was still charming, with its red tile floor and colorful carved chairs. A refresh to the window treatments and wall hangings wouldn't cost much and would give an updated feel.

The clients were mostly older, though. She and Trina were the youngest people in the place, by far. It was great they were catching the over-sixty crowd, but a restaurant needed to appeal to more than seniors to survive. She scanned the menu prices. Hmm, that explained why the fixed-income set liked the place, but if that was the restaurant's niche, they should be advertising for the teen and early-twenties crowd, too.

Interesting that the majority of the restaurant's patrons weren't Latino. Which didn't make sense, given the demographics of the area. Were the Quintanas skewing more Tex-Mex these days? Was their food getting less than authentic? She noted the questions down on her pad.

"Take your order?" The teen waiter, dressed in the black shirt and slacks the wait-staff had always worn, looked at them without a smile.

"So what's the best thing here?" Dale asked jovially.

The waiter shrugged. "I don't like Mexican food."

*Ouch.* "Uncle Dale, you should see if some of their foods are heart-healthy. Isn't that what your doctor said?"

He sighed noisily. "All right. Hit me. What's the healthiest thing on the menu?"

The waiter started to shrug, then seemed to notice that Veronica was listening. "I guess the taco salad," he said.

Molly frowned. Not only were taco salads an American innovation on Mexican food, but they were served in deep-fried shells and with heavy sauces. Popular, sure, but not a great choice if you were watching your cholesterol. "Okay if I order for you, Uncle Dale?"

"Order for me too, Mom, I don't know what I like." Trina eyebrows furrowed as she put down the lengthy menu.

Molly ordered different combination plates for all of them, with cups of soup to start. While they waited, they crunched on tortilla chips and salsa, the type that could be bought at any discount grocery store.

"You excited about school tomorrow, honey?" Uncle Dale asked.

"No." Trina slumped. "I wish it could be summer all year around."

"Do you think you can find your way around after today?" Molly studied her daughter, worry and love twisting together in her heart. Was this move the right thing to do? Would it help Trina with her anxiety and keep her away from kids who wanted to take advantage?

Trina shrugged and grabbed a tortilla chip. "It's not even as big as my last elementary school. That's not what I'm worried about."

Uncle Dale waved a hand. "You'll be fine, you're a good student, and the kids here are nice." He turned to Molly. "Next on your agenda, you're going to have to find an apartment."

Molly felt her stomach drop. "We do? But I thought—"

"I know. I was hoping you could stay with me for a few months, but I spoke to Lisa this afternoon."

Trina wrinkled her nose like something smelled bad, and Molly had to work to keep from doing the same thing herself. A vision of Mrs. Johnson, walking rapidly away from her and Javier, flashed before Molly's eyes, along with a memory of the alive-and-well gossip circuit Aunt Lisa had always participated in. "Aunt Lisa doesn't want us there?"

"I'm sorry, hon, but you know how she is. Said she might come home earlier than expected, and it wouldn't be a good idea for you to settle in."

Molly rubbed the back of her neck. What had seemed like a secure plan just a few days ago—a job, a place to stay for the first month or two—was starting to crumble.

Uncle Dale's forehead wrinkled. "I'm sorry. I'd love to have you move in permanently, but..." He trailed off and spread his hands, palms up.

"Don't worry about it." She patted his arm. His health problems were significant enough that he shouldn't face any added stress. If Aunt Lisa didn't want her and Trina there, then they couldn't stay. "We'll find a place. How hard can it be?"

"Well, that's just it. There aren't a whole lot of rentals in Arcadia Valley."

"I want to have my own room." Trina turned to Dale. "Once, Mom and I only had one bedroom and we had to share."

"Oh, now, we had fun." But uneasiness crept up Molly's spine. She didn't want to go back to those days when she hadn't known for sure she was going to make it as an entrepreneur. Trina needed security and stability.

"Here ya go." The waiter set dishes in front of them and then left without asking if the order was right or if they needed anything else.

"Okay," Molly said after the waiter was out of earshot, "we have to taste everything and give our honest opinions."

"Sounds great," Uncle Dale said, digging into a crunchy taquito.

As they ate, they quietly discussed the food and Molly took notes. The cold avocado soup was delicious, but some of the other food was less impressive.

"I always did like fajitas," Uncle Dale said, "and these are pretty good."

Molly took a bite and chewed. There was nothing wrong with the Americanized dish, but nothing distinctive about it, either. "Try some of this steak enchilada, Uncle Dale, but just a little. You shouldn't be eating a lot of red meat."

"There's a lot here," he said, slicing it open. "Mmmm, shredded beef. I like it."

"Too cheesy." Trina wrinkled her nose.

Molly had to agree, but as she made her notes, she felt concerned for the family. This restaurant had definitely gone in the direction of less authentic and fresh, and just at the time when people wanted the opposite.

"It's not bad," Trina said thoughtfully as they finished up. "It's just like Taco Nation."

"Being like a fast food isn't exactly our goal." Javier had come up beside them, striking in his white shirt and thin, dark tie. He was laughing a little, obviously not taking Trina's observation seriously.

Which was too bad, because Trina had a point.

Trina put her hands over her mouth. "I'm sorry! I didn't mean anything bad. I *like* Taco Nation."

"Don't be sorry." Javier smiled reassuringly at her. "We need people who will tell it like it is." He was every inch the benevolent owner being kind to a young, foolish visitor.

Telling him the truth about El Corazon wasn't going to be easy.

Before they could get into conversation, Veronica gestured him over to the hostess stand, waving some paperwork.

"You ever work things out with him?" Uncle Dale asked Molly once he was out of earshot.

Molly gave Dale a meaningful look. Trina didn't need to know about Molly's romantic history, limited as it was.

But Trina's teen radar was on full alert. "What did you have to work out with him, Mom?"

"She dated him all through her senior year," Uncle Dale said, cluelessly loud.

"You *did*?" Trina stared from Javier to Molly. "You never date anybody."

Trust a tween to tell the hard truths. "It was a long time ago and it's not important."

"You really ought to do some dating," Uncle Dale

said. "Any man would be lucky to have a sweet girl like you."

Dear, kind Uncle Dale. "Let's focus on final impressions of the food," Molly said. "What did you think of the gorditas?"

But they'd barely talked another minute when Javier pulled out the empty chair at their table and slid in with that Quintana grace that had always made Molly's breath catch. He smiled at Trina. "What did you think of the school? Did they make you feel welcome?"

"I like Raquel and Laura," Trina said, a little shy in a stranger's presence. "They were really nice."

"Petey's girls?" Uncle Dale asked.

Inside Molly, everything froze.

"Uh-huh," Javier said. "They're twelve and fourteen now."

Molly held herself very, very still. "What are their last names?"

"The Jones girls. You remember Mr. Jones, don't you?" Javier asked the question in a way that indicated he had no clue that he was raking Molly's heart into shreds.

"My old friend Petey Jones. Died too young." Uncle Dale shook his head and then turned to Molly. "Don't you remember him? He always brought you candy. Had a soft spot for you, it seemed."

There was such a loud, roaring sound in Molly's

ears that she could barely hear or process the conversation around her. But she had to. She had to know what she was dealing with, here. *Focus. Pay attention.*

"Since he passed," Javier explained, "I do what I can to help his wife. Mariana's my cousin, and she's struggled. She was so much younger."

"Young to be a widow," Uncle Dale agreed. "Good old Pete. Everybody liked him."

Molly had to swallow down the bile that rose in her throat. Forget about focusing and gaining information. More important that she keep herself from breaking down in front of her daughter. She wanted to leave the table, but she wasn't sure she could get her legs to support her.

"Mariana idolized the man," Uncle Dale said. "Didn't know what to do without him, to the point where I was worried about the girls."

"We all were," Javier agreed. "That's why some of her cousins have stepped in. Kept things going, especially since she had some surgery."

"I hear she's doing better. Doubt she'll ever marry anyone else, though. For her, he was the sun and moon."

*Enough.* Molly stood so fast she jolted the table. "Is your ladies' room still back there?" She gestured toward the center hallway, her hand shaking.

"Same as always." Javier's forehead wrinkled as he studied her. "You okay?"

She nodded, hurried across the dining room to the ladies' room, and promptly lost her dinner.

The sweet girls who'd befriended Trina were Mr. Petey's daughters. Molly leaned against the side of the stall, forehead sweating, neck damp. When she'd known the Joneses, they'd had only one child, a baby girl. That must be Raquel. Laura must have come along later, after Molly had left town.

Petey's widow was Javier's cousin. She'd known that, but she just hadn't put two and two together. The Quintanas' extended family was large, with dozens of cousins, aunts, and uncles. If she'd been curious about the rest of Mr. Petey's family—which she'd certainly suppressed, if she'd felt it at all—she would have been looking for a widow with one child, not two.

Now Trina was becoming friends with Petey's children. She reviewed the two girls in her mind, trying to figure out if they looked like their father.

Even the effort to picture Petey in connection with his daughters made Molly feel sick again.

She left the stall and washed her hands. Used damp paper towels to wipe her face and pat at the back of her neck.

Looked at herself in the mirror, met her own steady gaze.

Did she have any negative feelings about those girls, given her hatred of their father? *Please don't let me, Lord.*

But of course, she had practice overlooking one half of a child's genetic heritage. She did it every single day with her own daughter.

Trina. Petey's daughter, as well.

# CHAPTER THREE

J AVIER MADE SMALL TALK with Trina and Dale while they picked at a few remaining bites of dinner.

"How about if I take Trina home, give you and Molly a chance to talk?" Dale suggested. "You know, she's very good at what she does. She might be just the shot in the arm El Corazon needs."

"Mom does it everywhere she works," Trina said. "She got her picture in the paper twice when we were in Cleveland." She looked at him pleadingly. "I sure hope you don't cancel the job, Mr. Quintana. I like Arcadia Valley."

Javier blew out a breath. Despite his ambivalence about Molly, and about the circumstances of Trina's conception, he hated to do something that would hurt a young girl.

"And Arcadia Valley likes you," Dale boomed out. "Come on, princess, let's go on home and let your mother work her magic."

As Dale and Trina stood up, Molly returned to the table. "Ready to go?" she asked, looking relieved.

Dale held up a hand. "I'm going to take this young lady home so she can pick out her outfit and get her supplies ready for tomorrow. You stay here and talk as long as you need."

"It's a good idea for us to talk a little, if you have time," Javier added.

Molly bit her lip and reached out to brush back Trina's hair. "You okay with that, or do you want me to come help you?"

"I just have to do my backpack and figure out a shirt. You'll be home before I go to bed, right?"

"Of course."

As the two left, Molly's eyes followed her daughter, full of love.

Javier watched Molly and questions burned in his mind. *Who's Trina's father? Why did you cheat on me with him? What did he give you that I couldn't?*

Without realizing he was doing it, he was studying Molly closely, and now he saw that her eyes were a little red. "You sure you're okay?"

"I'm fine," she said, turning back to him. "Let's talk business." She held up her notepad, almost like a barrier.

She seemed so much less relaxed than she had earlier, when they'd first arrived. He tried to rewind their conversation and remember whether anything that had been said had upset her, but he couldn't think of what it would be. Maybe she'd gone off to the ladies' room to talk to a boyfriend and something was wrong.

Did she have a boyfriend?

*Business, business.* "Now that you've tried it, what do you think? Any problems with the food?" El Corazon had been founded on the notion of great Mexican food, food that warmed the heart. Thank heavens they still had that going for them.

She studied him a minute. "I took some notes."

"And? I don't want the restaurant to change, Molly. I want to keep up my parents' traditions."

"It's already changed. The food isn't as good as it was when I was a kid."

Angry heat flooded him. "What do you mean?"

"I mean that the food is one reason the restaurant isn't doing well. Probably the main reason. I can provide you with an initial analysis."

"What's wrong with the food?" He could hear himself talking too loudly. "What's your point of reference?"

"Javier. Please. I know you're having a hard time liking or trusting me, but you said you'd looked at my website. My customers have been unanimously satisfied and they found me fair to work with."

"Of course." Reluctantly, he acknowledged in his own mind that what she said was true.

"I'd need to observe a lot more, but right away, a couple of things struck me as problematic."

His jaw clenched, but he forced himself to relax and listen. "Like what?"

"Your wait staff. And some of the food."

"Who'd you have as a server? Dakota?" He frowned. He should have made sure this table got the best of service.

On the other hand, they were trying to find out what was wrong, how to attract more customers. Maybe he could learn something from what Molly said.

She nodded. "He wasn't exactly eager to help us. He said he doesn't like Mexican food."

Javier blew out a breath. "I need to work with him."

"Training might help." She sounded skeptical.

"We have a small pool to choose from," he said, feeling defensive. "A lot of the boys around here work the ranches for more money."

"I bet." She frowned. "What about the girls?"

"We usually stick to boys and men as the wait staff."

She raised her eyebrows. "You're kidding, right?"

He shook his head and reached for an explanation. "It's tradition. The uniforms. Everyone knows it, so no girls apply. I'm not breaking any laws."

"That's a pretty strong tradition, if the whole town knows girls needn't apply. Don't you want to double your pool of applicants? Girls can wear the exact same uniform."

"Thank you!" Veronica called from the other side of the room, where she'd just ushered out the last customers. "I've been telling him that for years."

It was true, she had. He just had an image of the restaurant in his parents' time, and part of the magic had been attentive, committed male waiters.

But not, he had to admit, slack, uninterested waiters like Dakota. That *did* need to change.

"What's wrong with the food?" He braced himself for the worst, and resolved inside he wasn't going to let her be hired if she were going to change El Corazon.

"There's a lot that's good," she said gently. "The chili greens and beans are wonderful. So is the cold avocado soup."

He breathed easier. "Thanks. The *sopa fria de aguacate* is Mama's recipe, and Maria suggested the greens and beans."

"I remember the soup." She met his eyes for a moment and then looked away. "It's great they're still using the same recipe. But what happened to her salsas? Didn't you used to serve both red and green?"

"Most of our customers prefer red these days." He did himself.

"What was served tonight seemed like it came from a jar."

"Right. Everyone does jarred salsa nowadays.

Saves on food bills."

She just shook her head. "Refried beans from a can… same rationale?"

"Yeah."

She propped her chin on her hand. "Javier, there are so many varieties of salsa now, even in the grocery store. You have to be all that and better, right? You should resurrect all your mom's old recipes and offer up some variety, give customers a choice. Home baked tortilla chips."

"What's the ROI?" he argued. "Where would we get the time and the workers for that?"

"You have to spend money to make money. If you don't, people who like fresher, more modern food will go to other restaurants in town. Like Uncle Dale. He remembers this place, but he doesn't come here as often anymore because he likes the food better at Fire and Brimstone."

Javier let out a disgusted snort. "That place doesn't even look like a restaurant! It's an old automotive garage!"

"Repurposing is chic," she said. "Have you tasted their food?"

"No, but I heard it's a total mishmash. Kimchee and barbeque on pizza? Really?"

"They have lines out the door every night."

Yeah. He'd heard the same thing. He frowned down at the same red tile floor that had always been there. "I'm not making El Corazon into a garage or warehouse. And I'm *not* changing its name."

"Of course not. El Corazon really *is* the heart of your family, so the name is perfect. Seems like the structure of the place is sound, so there's no reason to change the building at all. Although the décor could use some freshening up..."

"See ya, Javier." One of their cooks, Pablo, started out the door. "You coming?" he called back into the kitchen.

"Yeah, I'm ready." Maria followed Pablo, looking curiously over at Javier and Molly.

The cooks were interested, which only made sense. "What will they do if we make a bunch of changes?" he asked.

Molly shrugged, "I bet they'd jump up and down. Whoever made that avocado soup is a great cook and could make fresh salsa very well, I'm sure."

"We'd have to pay them for more hours, or hire someone else to prep."

She nodded. "There will be some expense."

"And some change," Veronica, the cash register drawer in her hands, stopped at the table. "We all know Javier hates change."

"Hey!" He held up a hand, protesting. His old-fashioned side was a family joke, but it had held them all together. Which was harder and harder to do, now that his parents were gone.

He didn't want to raise the question in his own mind, but Molly was doing that for him. Was his desire to stay traditional actually hurting his family's restaurant?

Veronica set down the money drawer and slid into a seat at the table. "If it's the cost you're worried about, don't. We already paid the down payment on the contract and Alex says he'll pay for the whole initial consult. We know you sank your savings into the cottages."

"No," Molly interrupted. "Javier runs this place. He has to agree or it won't work." She met his eyes and kept looking at him with a cool, steady gaze.

He could drown in those eyes. Emotions flooded him. He'd loved her so much that it hurt.

And that was even before she'd betrayed him.

"Javier." Veronica gripped his arm, pulling his attention back from Molly. "I think the alternative is closing down within a couple of years."

"It's not that bad yet! We're full every Friday and Saturday night!" Even as he said it, he knew in his heart the crowds weren't what they'd used to be.

"We need to fix it now. We don't want to keep watching it sink."

"I don't want to lose the traditions we were built on." He leaned back and crossed his arms.

"Like the mariachi music?" Veronica rolled her eyes and turned to Molly. "He won't let us play anything modern in here."

A smile tweaked the corner of Molly's mouth. Was she laughing at him?

Or was she remembering how he'd used to hum that music to her?

"You don't have to change all the traditions." Molly touched his hand, and a shot of warmth went directly to his heart. "You just need to create some new ones. You could even emphasize the restaurant's history on the menus. Pictures of your parents and their Mexican hometowns."

He frowned. She was making a reasonable argument, and it was just a consultation. If smart ideas were coming from anyone but Molly, he'd accept them, wouldn't he?

Which meant that, if he didn't, he was letting his high school history stand in the way of his family's success today.

"C'mere, Javier." Veronica stood and turned to Molly. "Do you mind if we talk privately for a minute?"

"Not at all. Should I go?"

"No, stay here. We'll just be in the kitchen." She grabbed Javier's arm and pulled.

He stood, and for just a minute, looked at Molly's downturned head. There was a little slump to her shoulders. It couldn't be easy, trying to sell yourself.

Especially to an old boyfriend.

He shook off the thought and followed Veronica into the kitchen.

As soon as they were out of earshot, Veronica turned to him. "You need to get over her. You haven't had a serious girlfriend since high school, and that blonde in there is why."

He hadn't been expecting a frontal attack on his personal life. "Veronica. Not your business."

"Yes, it is, because I care about your happiness. You know you want to have a family, and you're not getting any younger. You've let yourself become bitter toward women. It's nice you help out with Laura and Raquel, but don't you want children of your own?"

"Someday, sure, but—"

"So you need to work out your anger about what Molly did to you. You need to see that she's just an ordinary person who made some mistakes. Maybe then, you can move on with your life." She wrapped her arms around him in a quick hug, then stepped back. "Don't you see? This restaurant renovation is a golden opportunity for you to heal old wounds."

He opened his mouth to scold her for intruding and then closed it again.

Was she right? Was daily interaction with Molly Abbott the way to get past his feelings and open his heart?

"Not to mention that Daniel, Alex and I agree this is the right thing to do. You know Mama and Papa left the restaurant to all four of us, not just to you. By rights, we could force this on you. But we would rather convince you that this is the only way to save El Corazon."

"That's a little overdramatic—"

"Molly is the only person who knows its history. Our history and your history. She has great recommendations. She can help us if you'll let her!"

He blew out a breath. Thought about what it would be like to work with Molly on a daily basis for a few weeks.

Bad... and good.

But the image of closing down El Corazon was worse than bad. "Come on." He put an arm around Veronica and guided her back out to the dining room, then looked from Molly to Veronica. "All right. Molly can do the initial analysis. But that's all. Whether to implement the changes remains to be decided."

Veronica pumped her arm. "Yes!"

"Not so fast," Molly warned, hand in the air. "I'll need you to agree to some partial implementation. Some experiments. We have to adjust and test before deciding definitively what direction you should go."

He looked at her clear gaze and sighed. When had Molly Abbott gotten so determined, so professional? "If you'll run it by me first, all right. But I'm not going to agree to a bunch of big changes."

Veronica jumped up and hugged him. "Thanks,

Javie."

"You won't be disappointed," Molly said. "You'll see." She took her purse from the back of her chair and shrugged into a sweater. "Now, to find a short-term rental."

"You're not staying with your uncle?"

She shook her head. "Aunt Lisa put the kibosh on that."

Javier remembered the woman who'd treated Molly like a second-class citizen. "She hasn't changed, huh?"

"Nope." She turned to Veronica. "Know of any apartments for rent?"

MOLLY SAID GOODBYE to Javier and Veronica and gathered her things to leave El Corazon. She should have felt thrilled for Javier to agree to work with her, but she was too emotionally worn out for that.

The memories of horrible Mr. Petey had drained her. And yes, she'd figured his remaining family might live in town, but she hadn't considered that she—and, worse, Trina—would be in close contact with them. For Molly, it would be salt in a wound she'd thought had healed over. More worrisome, she feared damage to Trina, who only knew that her father hadn't been a good person, and that was why Molly was raising her alone.

She walked out into the parking lot and looked upward at a darkening sky that was starting to fill with stars. "I think you led me to come here, God," she whispered, "but if I misread that, shut the door. Protect me from evil and show me the next step on your path."

"Molly!" Veronica called from the open door of the restaurant. "I know the perfect place for you to rent!"

THE NEXT AFTERNOON, Molly and Trina pulled through a rustic arched gateway into the Valley Cottages. Immediately the road divided into a one-way circle, with widely spaced cottages on one side and a tree-shaded community area in the center. Molly had seen online that there were ten cottages in all, but only four were visible from the entrance.

Each small cottage had a front porch with a swing or Adirondack chairs. Trees shaded little yards that faded off into wilder landscape. Molly dimly remembered that the cottages had previously been vacation rentals, but apparently they'd evolved into semi-permanent residences.

"It's so cute!" Trina bounced around in the passenger seat.

"It is." Molly pulled to the side of the road to read a text message. "Let's see, Veronica's supposed to meet us at cottage seven. Help me look for it." She pulled back onto the road and drove forward, slowly.

"There." Trina pointed. "Oh, it's cute! But tiny. Will I have my own bedroom?"

"It's supposed to be two bedrooms, but remember, we're just looking. We haven't decided on this place yet."

"I just want to move where we're going to be already." Trina leaned back in the car and looked up at the ceiling. "I'm tired of having most of my stuff in boxes."

"I know. Me, too." Molly pulled into the cottage's short gravel driveway, turned off the car, and patted Trina's arm.

From next door, a man came out and down the steps.

Javier.

Javier? What was *he* doing here?

Slowly, Molly got out of the car. But Trina wasn't nearly as hesitant. "Hey, Mr. Quintana, do you live here?"

"Yes, I do." He cocked his head to one side. "Veronica told me someone was coming to look at this one. Since she had to go to the restaurant, she asked me to show it. Are you... Is that *you*, who are prospective tenants?"

Molly gulped. "Yes."

Her eyes looked into Javier's stormy ones and she

took a step back. He was *not* happy about this, and understandably so. She wasn't happy either.

"We need to talk," he murmured to her as they followed Trina up onto the porch. Then he flipped into what was obviously a practiced narrative, upping the volume so Trina could hear. "The cottages and yards are small, but you're welcome to use the community area in the center. That building is for parties, and there's a basketball court and a community garden."

Molly and Trina turned together to look. At the center of the round road, a grassy area held playground equipment, and a few young kids shouted as they played on it. On a bench, two women sat talking.

It looked to be a nice little community. Except for the worrisome presence of the first love she'd never really gotten over.

Javier unlocked the door and held it for them to walk in ahead of him. "It's small," he said, waving a hand around the main room. "No separate kitchen, just all one room."

But there was a table for two in front of a window, near the stove, refrigerator, and counter space that lined one side of the cabin's main room. The paneled walls gave the place a charming retro look.

"Bedrooms on this side." He said beckoned Molly to follow him. Simple white bedspreads and folded blankets topped the beds, and plain white curtains billowed and flapped as Javier opened windows.

"This bathroom is tiny!" Trina called.

Molly joined her in the old-fashioned, pink-tiled bathroom. Definitely not much room to move around, especially when Javier came into the doorway.

Molly drew in a breath and discreetly stepped back. He seemed to take up all the air in the little room.

"Mom! You're crowding me." Trina nudged Molly back toward Javier, causing her to bump against his broad chest. "I call the big shelf for my makeup."

Which consisted of mascara and lip-gloss, but whatever. "Um, fine. *If* we decide to take it." She looked up at Javier, trying to signal for him to move back. He stared down at her, his eyes serious and concerned. And gorgeous. "Could we take a look at the yard?" she asked, as much to escape the uncomfortable nearness as because she was seriously considering living here. Which she wasn't. Working with Javier was one thing, but to be his next-door neighbor in a tiny, open community like this would be asking for trouble. Surely there was somewhere else, although the paper had listed only two apartments, one very small and one almost all the way to Twin Falls.

The three of them headed out into the yard, and Molly looked back at the cottage. She could imagine the little porch with a pot of geraniums or a harvest display of pumpkins and hay bales. "Do people live here year round, or are they just short term?"

"Honestly, most people who move here end up staying awhile. It's a nice community. We have somebody come in and mow, and do the leaves, and clear snow. Places are small, easy to care for."

"And the Quintanas own the place?"

"Me and Veronica. We wanted to invest in Arcadia Valley."

"Hey," Trina said, "Hey, Laura!" She ran toward the street where a girl and her dog were walking.

"Trina! What are you doing here?" The two girls started talking, words tumbling over each other.

Molly's heart sank. The only thing worse than living next door to her still-angry ex-boyfriend was living down the street from the widow of the man who'd done his best to ruin her life. She glanced up at Javier. "Does *everyone* in your family live here?"

He laughed, a deep sound that played along Molly's nerve endings. "No, just me and Mariana and Veronica. So I guess we're creeping up toward a majority."

"Mom, she lives here!" Trina beckoned Molly closer. "That would be so awesome if we did, too."

"You could ride the bus with me and Raquel," Laura said as the overgrown puppy she was walking ran circles around her, tangling her in the leash. "Cowboy! Stop it!"

Trina laughed and knelt to help Laura untangle herself. "Can we, Mom? Please?"

"We'll see." Molly's stomach sank. "There are a lot of factors to consider."

Trina pouted.

"Come walk Cowboy with me and I'll show you around," Laura said to Trina. "Did you see what Xenia Smith was wearing today?"

And they were off, talking a mile a minute. Loud laughter followed as the puppy grabbed his own leash in his mouth and tugged.

"They've sure hit it off," Javier remarked, smiling fondly after the girls. His help and attention to his cousin's children touched Molly's heart. It wasn't every man who would take the time to forge a relationship with teenage relatives, especially moody girls.

"I'm glad of it," Molly said, shoving aside the implications of the girls' relationship, the fact that, biologically, they were half-sisters. "Thank you again for having your nieces help Trina when we first arrived in town. The shoes we bought that night turned out to be, *like, totally perfect.*" She mocked Trina as she smiled up at him.

Javier chuckled. "From what I hear, shoes are crucial."

Their eyes caught, and held.

*Wow.* Molly looked away toward the disappearing

tweens. "Although I think it's important for Trina to make a lot of friends, rather than putting all the pressure on your nieces. I'm going to make sure she gets involved in an activity or two. She did gymnastics last year, and worked on the yearbook."

"Good thinking." Javier's voice sounded neutral, businesslike, making Molly wonder if she'd imagined the undercurrents between them. "Is there anything else you'd like to see?"

"Ummmm..." She looked around, desperate for a distraction, and saw a fenced area beside the playground. "What's that?"

Javier followed her gaze and then touched the small of her back to guide her toward the fenced area. "Come on, I'll show you."

*Breathe.* This was terrible. She couldn't be falling hard for Javier again, could she?

"It's the community garden I mentioned before," he said a moment later as he opened the gate of the low picket fence. He ushered her inside. "Lots of people have vegetables getting ripe. I'm always getting giant zucchini on my doorstep. Not that I know what to do with them."

"You take them to the restaurant and use them!" Molly looked around the small, carefully tended plots with mounting excitement. "Look at the variety. Is any of this yours?"

Javier laughed. "I make a token effort, but I have a

black thumb. And I'm never here."

"Still. It's encouraging how well everything's growing here. If the farmers around here have this kind of range and productivity, it makes farm-to-table a real possibility."

Javier frowned. "We have suppliers we've been working with for decades."

"Mom!" Trina hollered, and the two girls ran up, breathless. "Laura has two more puppies at the house, and they're selling them. Can we get one?"

"No. Absolutely not." Molly smelled burgers grilling, a mouthwatering scent.

"Mo-om!"

"Just come look at them," Laura suggested. "They're really cute."

Molly couldn't think of an excuse, and Trina's eyes pleaded as if she were a puppy herself. "All right," she said, "just for a couple of minutes."

"Yay!" Trina crowed, hugging Molly hard, and then they all followed Laura toward a bigger cottage on the other side of the circle.

Inside, Mariana greeted them warmly. "Go with Laura and see the puppies," she said to Trina, and then turned to Molly. "You must all stay to dinner."

Molly was trying not to look too closely at Mariana, who'd aged noticeably since their occasional encounters years ago. "Oh, we can't do that. Uncle Dale is waiting for us. But that's really kind, thank you."

"At least come sit and have a little coffee, then."
Without waiting for an answer, Mariana bustled back
into the kitchen.

Molly could hardly refuse, especially since the two
girls, now joined by Raquel, had gone out back to
play with the dogs. But when she sat on the couch
opposite Javier, a photo on the end table stole away
her breath.

Petey, in a place of honor.

A place he really didn't deserve.

"That's my husband, but you knew him, didn't
you? You're Dale and Lisa's daughter, yes?"

*Don't give anything away.* "They're my aunt and
uncle, and they took me in when my parents were
killed." Molly swallowed, her hands sweating. "And
yes, I did know your husband. He was friends with
Uncle Dale."

"He spent so much time over there! As a new wife,
I sometimes got jealous!" Mariana laughed at herself.

Molly couldn't speak, overwhelmed with the
memories of Petey's frequent visits, his compliments,
his little gifts. Javier and Mariana started chatting, and
after a stern self-scolding, she forced herself to join in,
to drink her coffee. To smile and nod as Mariana
extolled the virtues of Valley Cottages.

The girls came back in, and Trina gave her another
pleading, puppy-dog look. "Can we take the cottage,

Mom? Please?"

She couldn't think of a reason not to live here. At least, not one she could share. She glanced over at Javier and couldn't avoid the concern and emotion in his eyes. "I need to think about it."

Her feelings for Javier had to remain secret. So did her ugly history with Mariana's dead husband.

Beneath the surface of the conversation, Molly felt the strings wrapping tighter and tighter around her.

# CHAPTER FOUR

I WANT VETO POWER over anyone who moves into the cottages." Javier held the door for his sister and then walked around to the drivers' seat. It was a beautiful late-August Saturday, warm but with the occasional falling aspen leaf hinting at autumn.

Veronica wanted to go to the farmers market. He had no interest, but he'd offered to drive her. It would give him a chance to talk to her.

"Too late," she said as he pulled out onto the highway. "Molly and Trina are moving in next week."

"What?" His muscles tightened and he banged a hand on the steering wheel. "When were you going to tell me that? When was *she?*" He'd seen both Molly and his sister every day this week. "Someone could have clued me in."

"They need a place to live, Javier." Veronica crunched up the wrapper on a granola bar and, after a glance at him, twisted to place it neatly in the trash bag. "It's perfect for them, at least for now."

Where would it end? The world as he knew it was

spinning out of control.

"Besides," she said, "I figured you'd overreact. I didn't want to give you the chance to talk Molly out of it."

"Why not? What investment do you have in her living right next door to me?"

"What's bothering you?" Veronica's voice was too innocent.

"You know as well as I do. It's bad enough I see Molly almost every day at the restaurant, but to have her and Trina as next door neighbors…"

"First of all, it's not finalized yet. She may still change her mind. But I hope not." Veronica put her feet up on the dashboard, nails blue, flip-flops green, and a sassy smile that said she knew exactly what the problem was. "She's a good person, Javier. And from what I hear, you really loved each other once."

Javier snorted. "I thought so. But I was mistaken."

"Did you ever work out what happened to end your relationship? Or at least talk about it? Daniel says…" She trailed off.

He changed lanes and accelerated a little too hard. "What does Daniel say?"

"That she left town and you went after her."

He made a noise in his throat but didn't deny what she'd said. It was the truth.

"And then she told you she never wanted to see you again."

"That's right." Against his will, Javier's mind flashed back to those awful days. How he'd gone to visit Molly at her aunt's house when she didn't show up at school for a couple of days. How her aunt had said she was sick and couldn't come to the door.

The next he'd heard, she'd moved to Ohio. He'd never forget his desperation, his efforts to contact her, the way he'd begged his parents to let him visit. They'd finally agreed to loan him the car during a school break, and he'd gotten her contact information from Uncle Dale.

When he'd arrived at the address Dale had given him, he'd had to read the sign on the large brick building twice: Center for Women and Girls: Help with Crisis Pregnancies. When he'd finally gotten a message to Molly and she'd come outside, the bump beneath her loose, flowing shirt had been unmistakable.

Yeah, he'd said some awful things, but what could you expect? He'd known the baby wasn't his, and he'd been shocked to discover that his sweet, innocent girlfriend had been cheating on him.

He'd never forget how she'd drawn herself up to her full five-foot-four, crossed her arms over her belly, and told him to get out of her and her baby's life.

"Slow down!" Veronica said. "The market's right up there. Haven't you ever been before?"

"As a matter of fact, no, I haven't." He slowed

down, forced himself to relax his muscles, and turned sedately into the market.

The place was filled with cars, trucks, and people carrying things to the large enclosed area off to the right. Kids kicked a ball around a field next to a picnic area.

He let the organized chaos distract him from more memories. How he'd gone back to see her again a couple of months later, when he couldn't get her off of his mind. How he'd driven there too fast, just like today, hoping against hope that it wasn't too late for them. He'd even had a ring in his pocket. Ready to forgive her and give her a second chance.

She'd refused to see him, and when he wouldn't leave, she'd sent down a rubber-banded packet of his letters to her. Unopened. With a post-it note on top saying that it was best they both moved on with their lives.

He had to assume that meant she was reconnecting with the father of her child.

His whole self skittered away from the pain of that memory, seared into his brain but covered over with years of hard work and responsibility and keeping very, very busy. He'd let it go, so he'd thought.

Until Molly had shown up here with a living, breathing, lovable child. Obviously single.

But that ugly history and his curiosity about why she'd betrayed him stood between them.

He got out of the car and followed Veronica toward the enclosure, listening to the rise and fall of the cicadas, the chirping and chattering of birds. August sun beat down on his shoulders and back, warming his tight muscles.

"Well, look who's here." Veronica waited for him and nodded her head toward the picnic tables.

There was Molly, the topic of his dreams and nightmares, her blond head bent over a notebook. Next to her was Maria. Trina sat across the table, a textbook open in front of her, highlighter in hand.

Longing pierced him. He'd wanted to have children with Molly at one time.

But then he came back to himself and held Veronica's arm, stopping. "Did you plan this, too?"

"No! I had no idea she'd be here." She smiled up at him, a dimple visible in her cheek. "But it would be rude not to say hello, wouldn't it?"

Javier glared at his little sister. "I don't guess we can avoid it, but I'm on to what you're doing, and I don't like it."

"Come on!" But as they started walking toward the trio, a middle-school-aged girl stopped beside their table and spoke to Trina. Trina looked up, and when she saw who it was, smiled warily.

The girl spoke rapidly and gestured toward the enclosed part of the market. Trina spoke to her mother, a strange expression on her face. Right. This was the girl who headed up the so-called mean team.

He wondered why she seemed to be inviting Trina, a new girl, to do something. But Molly nodded at the other girl, smiling, seeming oblivious. Trina got up slowly and went off with the girl, shooting a look back at her mother.

Odd.

He smelled an old familiar smell, popcorn and sugar, and noticed a kettle corn stand beside the entrance to the farmers' market. The girls headed toward it. People jostled him, crowding toward the entrance with bushels and crates of produce.

"Hey, Molly, Maria!" Veronica greeted the women, and they both turned and smiled. When Molly looked back and saw Javier, though, her expression darkened.

Well, that was understandable. It was how he felt, too, especially after his conversation with Veronica that had dredged up all kinds of memories.

"Hey," Maria greeted them with a smile and then went back to looking at the tablet computer.

"Just the people I wanted to see." Molly stood and hugged Veronica. Then, after a second's hesitation, she shook Javier's hand. "I want to show you what we've been working on."

So it was all business. Of course. She hadn't been inside his head. No memories were stirring for her, or if they were, they weren't painful ones.

She took the tablet from Maria, scrolled and clicked until she'd pulled up a list. "Look," she said, "here are all the possibilities for fresh produce. I've listed it out by month. Now, this is preliminary, I still have to talk to more of the farmers, but it looks like there's plenty to build from, for farm to table Mexican."

"We could definitely make the changes she's suggesting," Maria added, her voice hesitant. "Pablo and I discussed it, and we think we can make it work."

They did?

Javier pretended to look at the list, but he was more captivated by Molly's excitement. He remembered her like that. When she'd gotten excited about a class or a movie or a party, she'd never been able to hide it.

That was just one of the things he'd loved about her. It was just too bad she'd gotten equally excited about some other guy.

"When I found out Maria was the one who'd made the avocado soup and the greens and beans, I asked if she'd consult with me a little more today, and she agreed."

Javier frowned.

"Molly's paying me from her consultant budget," Maria said quickly. "But I'd do it for free. You and your family have been so great to me, and I want to give back, to help El Corazon."

Maria had started working at the restaurant just a year ago, so Javier didn't know her nearly as well as he knew Pablo. Still, how had he not realized one of his cooks had ideas to improve El Corazon?

He tuned back into the conversation between Molly and Veronica.

"So once I saw the possibilities, I mocked up a new menu, with Maria's help. It's not finished, but this is what it might look like." Molly scrolled and clicked again, then handed him the tablet.

Javier sat down, leaned back against the picnic table, and shaded the tablet with his hand so he could study it.

There was a lot of white space. In the center, just five or six appetizers, maybe eight main courses. About half were familiar, and the other half he'd never seen nor tasted before.

Molly and Maria were looking at him, and Veronica was reading over his shoulder.

"You'd do descriptions of the dishes, right?" Veronica asked.

"Yes, this is just a start. Look, I know it's really different from your menu now." She held up one of their current menus—when had she picked that up?—and the contrast was huge. While their current menu had at least fifty items on it, the new one she was suggesting had only maybe fifteen, total.

"People want choices. This…" He held up her

tablet. "This doesn't have any selection."

"It would change seasonally, maybe even more often depending on what's fresh and available. Restaurants are moving away from offering everything under the sun, because, if you do that, you have to rely on a lot of canned and frozen food. This simpler type of menu lets you work with the land and the seasons, with what local farms have available."

"It would be great to take more advantage of the farmers market," Maria added. "It's so much healthier. And the fresh produce tastes so much better when it hasn't travelled thousands of miles and sat in storage for weeks."

"It makes sense," Veronica said, her voice thoughtful. "It would be a big change for us, but maybe it's worth a try."

All three women looked up at him with similar expressions, various mixtures of hope and anxiety.

But he was still in charge of the restaurant. He knew his clientele, and this was just too big of a change.

"No. This won't work." Javier set the tablet down on the table a little too hard. "I'll be in the truck."

MOLLY WATCHED JAVIER stride off. Her fists clenched and her eyes filled. How could he negate all their work with just a few words?

She turned in time to see Veronica and Maria sharing an eye roll, obviously not surprised by Javier's reaction. "Will you watch my stuff for a minute?"

"Sure, but do you really want to..." Maria's brown eyes held concern.

She stood up. "I really do."

"Of course we'll watch your stuff." Veronica patted her arm. "We'll be here for you when he's bitten your head off."

She hurried after Javier, and caught up with him just as he reached his truck. "Javier!"

He opened the truck door and then turned. "Yeah?"

There was hot emotion in his eyes, too. Why?

"Look," she said, "if you're not going to listen to anything I say, I may as well just take the payment in the backout clause and leave now."

"Maybe you should." His dark eyebrows drew together.

She stared at him, remembering when those eyes had held warmth and love and caring. Caring that had meant the world to her, until it had exploded in a barrage of angry words and name-calling. Already raw from what she'd gone through with Petey, she'd been crushed. She'd had to shut herself off from him, for her own sake and for her baby's.

Now, though, she was fighting for Trina a different way. "Is that what you want? For me to leave, so you can stay in control?"

He lifted his chin and pressed his lips together, stifling who knew what sharp reply.

She pressed on. "Your family's restaurant is going downhill. You're not willing to try something new?"

"Look, Molly," he said, concern in his voice. "You've got to understand that when you spring such a big change on me—on our customers—it's not likely to work. This is a small, conservative town."

She studied him as her dream of building a life here started to fray. "I don't think that's true. Arcadia Valley isn't conservative. You are. You've closed yourself off from anything new. I'm sorry to see it." She spun away and hurried back toward the table, drawing in fast, shaky breaths, blinking away tears.

When she reached the table, and sat down, Veronica patted her shoulder. "Maria had to run. And don't worry about Javier. He'll come around. He's just being the bossy big brother. I just wonder..." She paused. "I wonder what happened between the two of you, to upset him that much?"

Her question made it clear that Javier hadn't spread the news of her supposed infidelity and disgrace to his family. Although somehow, the fact of Molly moving away due to a pregnancy seemed to be common knowledge in the town of Arcadia Valley. She'd seen the curiosity in people's eyes, especially during the event at the middle school.

The real story of what had happened would never be public knowledge if Molly could help it. She had to protect her uncle and her daughter. "It's a long story." Molly sighed. Veronica meant well, but a change of subject was in order. "Have you seen Trina?"

"She's over by the door into the market, with Xenia Smith."

"That girl who was here?" Molly squinted in that direction and saw Trina. "Are they talking to boys?"

Veronica nodded. "I've been watching them. That Xenia can be trouble."

Molly's stomach went from woozy to upset in an instant, her protective-mother radar sensing something to watch out for. "What kind of trouble?"

"Well, she has a single mom for one thing."

Molly lifted an eyebrow. "So does Trina."

Veronica looked stricken. "Oh, my gosh, I'm sorry! What an awful thing for me to say."

"It's okay." Molly kept her voice neutral. She'd run into that attitude occasionally, but it was rare. She was surprised Veronica held it.

"Oh, wow, I didn't mean all single moms have bad families, obviously. You seem to do such a great job with Trina." Veronica clutched Molly's arm. "I'm sorry."

"No problem. Really, it's okay."

"But you should see this mom. She has a personal training studio and a figure that's obviously man-made. And a boyfriend of the month."

Molly bit her lip, torn between not wanting to gossip about another single mom, and wanting to know what kind of friends Trina was making. If Xenia's household was chaotic, Molly couldn't allow Trina to spend time there.

"I should just shut my mouth," Veronica said. "I'm a terrible gossip but I'm trying to get better."

Molly had been watching Trina, Xenia, and the boys, so she noticed when Trina stiffened and frowned. "Trina doesn't look happy."

"No, she doesn't."

Molly stood and waved until Trina saw her. She beckoned to her daughter and pointed at the table, indicating for Trina to come back.

After a little hesitation and talk, Trina and Xenia sauntered back toward them. Molly was about to scold Trina for being slow to obey when she saw her daughter's worried face.

"So, Trina said you're fixing up El Corazon," Xenia said with a surprising confidence given that she was in the same grade as Trina. "My mom and I are vegans. What do you have for us?"

Molly lifted an eyebrow, but she saw Trina silently begging her not to tangle with Xenia. "You make a good point," she said to the girl. "It's important to cater to people with special dietary needs. Thanks for mentioning it."

"How come you're vegans?" Veronica asked.

Xenia patted her flat stomach. "Mom says it's a good way to keep the weight off. Boys don't like fat girls."

Molly pressed her lips together. Why would any mother contribute to her daughter developing body-image issues?

Veronica stood. "Come on, Trina. I'll show you the pastries Raquel and Laura like best. Nice to see you, Xenia."

Molly caught the hint of hurt in Xenia's eyes, just before she sneered and strode away. The poor kid. Maybe she and Trina could have her over sometime, try to give her a hand.

She stared at her tablet. It was hard to know what to work on, now. Was she going to have to pull up stakes and leave, after all?

Her buzzing phone was a welcome distraction, until she heard Uncle Dale's worried voice. "Hey, sweetie," he said. "I've got bad news."

"What's that? Are you okay?"

"I'm fine, fine." He cleared his throat. "But Lisa called."

Molly swallowed down the slightly sick feeling she got when she heard her aunt's name. "Is something wrong?"

"She's coming back earlier than expected. Tomorrow night, in fact. So, it would be better if you and Trina could move out your things before she gets there." He paused. "I hate to do this to you, but she's so sensitive, and you know how she is when she's upset. I wouldn't want her to say something to hurt you or Trina."

That ship had already sailed. "I understand. Of course, we'll get out of there by tomorrow morning." Whether to go to the new cottage or to hit the road, she didn't know. She hadn't signed the rental agreement yet, so she wasn't locked into anything. If Arcadia Valley and El Corazon weren't going to work out, there was still time to change her plans.

She stared up at the blue sky, feeling the sun warm on her face. Should she just leave? Had coming home to Arcadia Valley been the wrong thing to do?

Going somewhere else, finding a job as a cook or caterer, would be the path of least resistance. But she wanted to raise Trina in Arcadia Valley. She wanted to do her consulting work on her own schedule, so that she could be here for her daughter and for Uncle Dale, once Aunt Lisa lost interest again and left him to fend for himself.

She'd made this plan for good reasons, and she needed to keep reminding herself of that. She couldn't back off without a fight. But how?

She looked out toward the parking lot. Javier's truck was still there.

She sat quietly, thinking and praying, and when a plan finally came to her, she headed across the parking lot to eat crow and see if Javier would cooperate.

# CHAPTER FIVE

"MOM, YOU SHOULD wear something nicer!" Trina stopped grating cheese and studied Molly with a twelve-year-old's critical eye. "Wear that blue flowered dress."

"I'm not wearing a dress." Molly checked the recipe Pablo had written out for her and then gave a final stir to the vegetables she was to fold in to appetizer quesadillas. "This is business, not social."

"Yeah, but you're trying impress Mr. Quintana. I don't think you should wear jeans."

"Miss Fashion. What should I wear, then?"

"Here," Trina said. "You pack this up, and I'll pick out a shirt."

"Don't dig in the boxes," Molly called after her daughter. "We don't want to have to repack, if this doesn't work." *But please, God, let it work.*

Twenty minutes later, they were carrying bags of food down the circle road to Veronica's cottage. Rather than argue, Molly had put on the pretty, sleeveless white shirt Trina had picked out for her, with light blue capris.

"Mom, I really hope this works. I like it here and I want to stay. Although Laura was kind of mean to me today. She said…" She paused.

"Are you okay? Is it something you need me to intervene with?" Molly knew how up and down middle school friendships could be—and how important to a girl. She'd step in if necessary, maybe mention something to Mariana or Javier. But she wanted to give Trina a chance to solve the problem herself.

Adding another layer of complication was that, unbeknownst to Trina, Raquel, and Laura, they were half-sisters. But she pushed that fact out of her mind for now.

Trina shrugged. "I don't *think* I need help."

Underneath the words, Molly sensed a concern Trina didn't want to voice. "Well, her mom seemed really happy that you're coming over to dinner. Come on, let's drop off our stuff on Veronica's porch and I'll walk across to Laura and Raquel's with you." She glanced sideways at Trina. "If there's any problem, you can always eat with us at Veronica's place. We'd love to have you."

"Right, that would be fun." Trina's expression went sarcastic.

As they approached Laura and Raquel's house, Raquel came out on the porch with one of the puppies. "Hey!" she called to Trina. "Come help me train Tripod."

"See you, Mom!" A big grin crossed Trina's face and she ran to Raquel without a backward glance.

Molly smiled despite the little tug at her heart. It was good Trina was making friends. It was good she was growing more independent of Molly, even if the independence was spotty. But she couldn't help feeling a little bit of longing for the days when Trina had hugged and kissed her goodbye.

She walked back over to Veronica's in a thoughtful mood. She'd been working hard with Pablo and Maria to plan out a wonderful menu with traditional and updated elements. This meal for Veronica and Javier was the last-ditch effort to convince them that her ideas could work for El Corazon. Everything was going to be fresh, top drawer, and delicious.

But given how traditional Javier could be, she wasn't counting on success. She and Trina had moved their things into the little cottage, but they'd only unpacked a few essentials. If need be, they could load up and move somewhere else.

She knocked at Veronica's door and then saw the note tacked to it. She put down her boxes and read. "Had to go help a friend in crisis, but make yourself at home. Javier will be over at six."

Her heart sped up its pace as she hesitantly let herself in. A meal for Veronica and Javier was one thing. A meal just for Javier was another.

It wasn't only that he was likely to be critical. It was the way their alone times brought up happy, carefree days.

What would her life have been like if those days hadn't been stolen from her? If she and Javier had gone forward with their innocent plans to marry? Would they have had two children by now? Three?

But of course, neither of those children would be Trina, and Molly wouldn't give up her daughter for any amount of romantic happiness, any other child. Trina was the joy that had come from her great sorrow, and she would never forget the lesson God had taught her through that experience.

His ways were mysterious, but wonderful as well.

She pulled containers out of bags and rummaged through the cupboards of Veronica's small kitchen. There was every pot, pan, and bowl imaginable, but they all looked unused. Veronica had told Molly she wasn't much of a cook.

Pablo and Maria had done most of the prep work, so putting things together went quickly. There was a lot of food. Had they made a mistake, creating an elaborate, multi-course meal?

But no. It was her last chance to convince Javier to let her do her magic at El Corazon. She had to go all out.

She hoped it would work, she mused as she sautéed wild shrimp. But she couldn't assume she knew better than God. Life had taught her that her own view of the world was clouded, and that only the Lord could see clearly.

She was just heating the quesadillas when there was a knock on the door, and Molly's heart fluttered as if she were a teenager with a date for the prom.

And why had *that* image come to her mind? By prom time, she'd been pregnant and living far away. Javier had probably taken someone else to the dance.

She rubbed her hands down the sides of her capris and opened the door.

Javier stood on the other side looking as self-conscious as she felt. "Where's Veronica? Her car isn't here."

"Come on in, hi. Veronica left a note." She showed it to him. "So... we can cancel if you want to, but Pablo and Maria and I already had all the food made, so..."

"Do *you* want to cancel?" His brown eyes pinned her.

"Well... sort of, because this is a little awkward, but... no. I really want to talk you into letting me do this thing."

"All right." He came into the kitchen and lifted an eyebrow when he saw the table set for one, with a kale, radish, and charred onion salad, black bean vinaigrette on the side. "But one condition. I can't eat this alone. You have to join me."

"There's no need of that. I already know what everything tastes like. I want you to be able to focus—"

"It's my condition," he interrupted. "Or we'll cancel."

That was Javier. He wanted what he wanted and didn't mind saying so.

"Controlling much?" she murmured as she obediently dished out a bowl of salad for herself.

Javier's mouth quirked up just a little. "That's what Veronica says."

"You've always been that way." She didn't add that there was a part of her that liked it. When Javier was in control, you knew you were safe.

They both sat down at the table, and their eyes met. Immediately, she flashed back on a night he'd scraped together money to take her to dinner at one of the nicer restaurants in Twin Falls. When she'd asked what the occasion was, he'd told her they'd been dating six months.

She'd known that, but hadn't wanted to make a big deal of the anniversary. The fact that he'd remembered had touched her heart. He'd been so much warmer and more emotional than most high school boys, and she'd loved it.

Now, he reached for her hand, and her heart soared like a kite on the wind. Oh, she had it bad. It would take him about five minutes to draw her right back in his arms again.

His fingers tightened on hers. "Will you pray with me?"

Oh. "Of course." She lowered her head and offered a silent apology to God for being disappointed about the reason Javier wanted to hold her hand. Praying together was more important than playing at romance.

When the prayer was over, she reminded herself of why she was here. Not to rekindle their relationship; that had been a silly little digression on her part. "Try this vinaigrette," she urged. "It's a black bean reduction."

"What's the green stuff?" He poked at his salad.

"Baby kale. It won't bite."

"I don't think I ever ate anything this green in my life."

She laughed at him. "Don't worry, it's not strong flavored. You *have* learned to eat salad, haven't you?"

"If there's no other choice." He grinned. "You know I'm a taco kind of guy."

"We have those, but only if you finish your salad."

"Now who's controlling?"

They were both smiling and then they weren't. It was as if they'd both realized what they were doing at the same time.

Joking. Flirting. Acting like this was a date.

"This is good, for salad," he said after a few bites.

"Not very traditional, though."

"There are all kinds of traditions in Mexico, right? Some kind of salad is part of a lot of them, even if it's just lettuce and tomato. Think of the kale as lettuce…"

Then, to avoid watching him as he ate, she got up and flipped the quesadilla, then slid it onto a cutting board and cut it. A little fresh salsa and guacamole on the side, and…

"Voila," she said, putting a plate in front of each of them. "You can't say *this* is untraditional."

"It looks good. But different." He took a bite, chewed it. "What's in it?"

"First of all, it's made with heirloom corn tortillas. Also, in addition to the vegetables and cheese, there are squash blossoms."

"Flowers?" He looked like he was going to choke. "I'm eating flowers?"

"Not just any flower, squash blossoms. They're trendy, but they've been eaten in Mexico for hundreds of years. I researched it."

He took a bite, then another. "It's good," he admitted.

*Whew.* She dared to look away from him and nibbled at her own quesadilla. Yes. She'd done okay with Pablo's recipe.

Javier put his fork down. "I still don't understand why this job is so important to you."

She wiped her mouth with her napkin and pushed her plate away. "Like I said, Trina needs to be in a more wholesome environment. I can't think of a place more wholesome than Arcadia Valley. It's a small school, warm church, good people." *At least, now that the one bad seed of the town, Petey, had passed on.*

"Okay," he said, "but there are a lot of small towns that match those criteria. Why here?"

She nodded, and since he was done with his plate, she cleared it, even though she hadn't eaten but a few bites herself. "It's Uncle Dale. I suspected this might be the case, and just today we got some test results. His heart's not good, and Aunt Lisa…" She paused.

"Your aunt can't take care of him? Veronica said she was coming home."

"She's coming home for a little while. Mostly to make sure Trina and I don't set up shop in her house. She'll leave again, and Uncle Dale will need help." As she spoke, she warmed corn tortillas and dipped up rice and beans. "They're the only family I've got."

"I'm surprised you didn't come back earlier, then, when she was small."

Her hands stilled in the process of putting tacos together, and she closed her eyes for a moment, trying to block out the images of Petey. She hadn't even considered returning until she'd gotten news of his death. "There were… reasons." She finished his plate and brought it over. "There you go. Wild shrimp, jicama slaw, and avocado creama tacos. You tell me if you've ever tasted anything better in your life."

"Bring your plate over and eat with me."

"Sure, okay." Still shaken from thinking about Petey, she dropped a shrimp on the floor and spilled cheese shreds over the counter.

She cleaned up, sat, and risked a glance at him.

He was watching her. "It looks delicious, Molly." He paused. "Look, I'm sorry I was so abrupt the other day."

"It's me who should apologize. I was pushing too hard, going too fast."

He took a couple of bites. "They're good. It's all good. But Molly." He put down his fork and wiped his mouth. "We need to talk about what happened when we were in high school. Clear the air, or it's going to keep getting in the way of our working together."

She seized on his last words. "You're leaning toward us working together?"

"I'm considering it." He leaned forward, elbows on knees. "Was it something I did that made you leave me?"

The question hung there between them.

"Molly?"

She reached for his hand and looked into his warm brown eyes. "No. You didn't do anything wrong. You were the best. The only..." She broke off, bit her lip, and pulled her hand back.

"Then why didn't you at least explain? Instead of just leaving? Molly, you meant everything to me."

"I wanted to, I... It just wasn't possible." She couldn't look at him anymore. "Could we drop this, please?"

"It wasn't possible because you were pregnant?" he asked gently.

She pushed her plate aside and stared at the table, heat rising to her face. She remembered the humiliation as if it had happened last week. The shock and trauma of the assault, the shattering of her dream of purity, the stunning fact that she'd become pregnant and was going to have a child at seventeen.

An awful, abusive man's child.

The Center for Women and Girls in Cleveland, where Aunt Lisa had sent her, had been a huge blessing in her life. A wonderful pastor and a couple of counselors later, she'd come to the place where she knew she could raise Trina, not blaming her for her father's sins. And from the first moment she'd held her innocent baby in her arms, love had overwhelmed her. There had been difficulties with raising a child alone, sure, but they'd made her lean hard on the Lord. In the end, so much good had come of it.

"Who was it, Molly?" Javier asked, his voice low and urgent.

Should she tell him? But Petey was Laura and Raquel's father, Mariana's esteemed husband. Not only that, but the one person in Arcadia Valley she'd told—Aunt Lisa—had slapped her repeatedly and insisted that if she wasn't lying, then she'd led on the much older family friend.

Only days later, she'd been shipped across the country, losing her home, her family, and her friends.

Losing Javier.

But Aunt Lisa had been right about one thing: no one in Arcadia Valley, especially Javier, would have believed her then.

She realized, now, that she should have gone to the police anyway. At the time, she lacked the confidence, knowledge, or strength.

As she'd matured, she'd agonized over whether to open up a case now. DNA testing would have proven Petey the father, and he'd have had to pay child support. More importantly, he might have been stopped from assaulting other innocent girls.

But a little quiet research had let her know that Petey's health had declined. He'd been too ill to keep up his evil ways, or at least, she'd hoped so.

Opening up a public case that would reveal the assault—and bring into question whether she'd consented or not—would have hurt Trina.

A gentle finger brushed tears from her cheek. She opened her eyes to find Javier kneeling beside her.

He touched her chin. "It didn't work out with him?"

She shook her head, hard.

"Are you sorry it happened, or did you want to leave me?"

The warmth and hurt in his brown eyes took her breath away. When she could, she gasped out, "Oh, Javier... I loved you so much."

Instantly he rose to pull a chair next to hers. "I loved you too, Molly. What happened broke my heart." He pulled her to him and she rested her head on his chest, feeling the strong heartbeat beneath her cheek.

They'd sat like this so often, and to Molly, who'd missed out on a loving family after her parents' death, the warmth and caring had been like water to a parched desert plant. She'd thrived on it.

She'd been with no one since, so once again, her skin craved his touch.

His arms tightened around her. "I can forgive what happened, if you forgive me for all the things I said to you when I came after you in Cleveland."

"You were shocked to find me... like I was. I understand your reaction now."

"Can you tell me...." He broke off.

"Tell you what?" But she knew, with a sinking heart, what he was going to say. He was proud, and honor was important to him. He would want to know.

Could she tell him some of it? At least, that what had happened had been against her will?

But knowing Javier, he wouldn't settle for half an answer. He'd want to know who had done it, what exactly had happened. He'd either get outraged on her behalf, or worse, outraged at her, if he didn't believe what she said.

Having him question her morality and accuse her of leading Petey on... that, she couldn't face. It was better not to know. "I'm sorry." She pulled away to look at him. "I just can't tell you."

Hot anger flashed into his eyes. He scooted his chair back and stood, spun away, and paced across the room to look out the window. "I don't understand."

*And with God's help, you never will.* "I'm sorry."

He came back over to the table and stood above her, and she couldn't look at him. The past was destroying her present-day plans, but she couldn't figure out how to stop that.

Tired. She was so tired. "I'll clean this up," she said mechanically. She stood and started picking up plates.

He would never accept her as a consultant. He would never get over the past.

He stood, arms crossed, watching as she took the dishes to the counter. Sliding past him, she made sure not even their clothes brushed together. She began to wash the dishes, to find storage containers for all they hadn't eaten. She'd leave it in Veronica's refrigerator, some good food for her friend to eat.

When she was finished, she gathered her bags and walked to the door. "I'm sorry it didn't work out, but thank you for at least giving me a chance."

"Molly." He lifted his hands, palms up. "I'm not saying you can't work with us."

Hope fluttered in her chest, a bird taking wing. "You're not?"

He shook his head. "The meal was delicious, and a lot of people would love food like that. It's obvious you have something to offer El Corazon. I'm not sure it will work, but since my brothers and sisters want you and trust you to improve things, you can try."

She swallowed, torn between delight and sorrow. "We can stay here in the cottages?"

He nodded. "Yes."

She started to step toward him and he held up a hand. "You can stay and do the work," he said, "but I... Look, I can't have any kind of friendship with you. It's strictly business."

The rejection hit her like a physical blow. "I understand," she managed to say as she let herself out.

She made it halfway to her cottage before she burst into tears.

THE NEXT TUESDAY AFTERNOON, Javier was repairing the sign in front of El Corazon when a compact car pulled into the parking lot. His brother Alex unfolded himself from the passenger side of the car, then went around to kiss the driver.

Who'd have ever thought Alex, the celebrity baseball star, would be riding shotgun in such a tiny car? Who'd have thought he'd be waving as it pulled away, with a sappy smile on his face? Jealousy pinged at Javier's heart, because he knew he'd never have anything like what Alex had found.

After the car disappeared down the highway, Alex loped over. "What're you doing, man?"

"Trying to patch this old thing together until our new sign comes in. Which you'd know if you ever got your eyes off your girlfriend and took a look at how the restaurant is doing."

"Whoa!" Alex stared at him. "What's got you in a mood?"

"I'm not in a mood." At least, nothing worse than usual now that Molly was back in town.

"Don't tell me you don't like the new sign idea? We all agreed on that a couple of months ago, before your problem person ever showed up on the scene."

So the link between his bad mood and Molly's arrival was obvious to his siblings. Great. "I like it fine. I'll be glad not to wrestle with this dinosaur anymore." He twisted a new lightbulb into the corner of the sign and flipped the switch, only to have two other bulbs pop and darken.

"Then what's bothering you?" Alex started unscrewing the burnt-out bulbs. "You jealous of me and Patricia?"

That cut too close. Javier pounded Alex on the back, just a little harder than he needed to. "I'm glad for you, man. You got the last trustworthy woman out there."

Alex grinned. "I scored the best, that's true. But..." His face went serious. "I don't agree about her being the last good woman out there. What about Molly?"

Javier snorted as he handed a box of bulbs to his brother and went to work on the sign's broken plastic corner. "I wouldn't set myself up for disappointment from her again, no way, no how."

Alex glanced over. "I was pretty young when all that happened, but come on, man. So she made a mistake."

"She disrespected me back then, and she's still doing it."

Alex lifted an eyebrow. "You respecting *her*?"

Javier looked down the road and spotted a welcome distraction. The school bus chugged toward the restaurant. It stopped in front, and the door opened.

Suddenly, Javier remembered getting off the bus at the end of a long, dull school day. Busy as their mother had been, she'd always stood waiting in the doorway of El Corazon, ready to hug them. Then she'd ask about their day, and scold them if they'd gotten into any trouble, and offer up spiced watermelon or mango before shooing them off to an empty corner of the dining room to do their homework.

He glanced toward Alex and saw him look from the bus to the restaurant doorway, undoubtedly remembering the same thing. In fact, Javier thought he saw his macho, athletic brother knuckle a tear from his cheek. As the youngest, he'd been their mother's pet and had taken her loss the hardest.

Javier looked away to give Alex space and saw Molly's daughter Trina exit the bus and rush into the restaurant, her face flushed.

"She looks upset," Javier said.

"Go after her, man," Alex's voice was rough. "Molly might need some help. I'll finish up here."

Which was code for *leave me alone*. Javier clapped his brother on the shoulder and went inside.

The last thing he expected to smell was his mother's beef and vegetable soup. They rarely served it at the restaurant; that was home food, not something to serve to customers. Or maybe Javier was wrong about that, because "Mexican Beef Soup/Caldo de Res" was listed on the new A-frame chalkboard that stood in front of the dining room door.

Where had that basket of peaches and apricots

come from? They had to be fresh, judging by the bright, fruity fragrance. But that didn't account for the amazing scent wafting from the kitchen.

"I don't want to talk about it!" Trina's voice came from the kitchen. "I'm starving! Get me food!"

Molly's voice was a murmur, and then Trina's begrudging "Sorry, Mom" drifted from the open kitchen door.

He heard the oven door open, and the sweet smell got stronger. Cookies? Chocolate chip? Javier's mouth watered, but he forced himself to wait a few minutes before strolling into the kitchen doorway to check out what was happening.

And there were Trina and Molly, a plate of cookies between them, a glass of milk for Trina and a cup of tea for Molly. Trina swiped her finger across Molly's phone and held it up. A smile spread across Molly's face.

Teen tantrum averted, at least for now.

Veronica came in the back door, followed by Alex, and the place got busy. Molly studied something on her tablet and then showed it to Veronica and Alex, and Trina pulled a fat textbook from her backpack and settled down at the business desk at the side of the kitchen. Maria rushed in, apologizing for being late, something about her mother. She went directly to the refrigerator, got out vegetables, and took them to the chopping block.

The place bustled; everyone busy but also having a good time. Molly was lively, quick to laugh, and she and Maria seemed to have struck up a nice friendship. Alex and Veronica worked together as a smooth team.

He'd never been the fun one and he wasn't now. As soon as he walked the rest of the way into the kitchen, everyone stopped laughing and focused on work. Which was good, because their first couple of dinner customers came in.

Pretty soon they had a nice little dinner rush and there was no time to joke or be cranky or sad. Even Trina helped when the dishes backed up. And Javier did his best to ignore Molly.

After the rush was over and cleanup began, he overheard Molly talking to Veronica. "The fresh-baked tortilla chips were pretty popular, huh?"

"People loved 'em. Everyone kept asking for more."

Molly studied the leftover bowls of them. "We still made too many, though. We don't want people eating so many chips they don't order much dinner. That's not going to help your bottom line."

"It all depends on how many customers we have." Veronica went back out to the front.

Looking thoughtful, Molly bagged up what was left of the tortilla chips. Then she poured what remained of a large bowl of fresh salsa into a plastic bottle. When she put it all into a big shopping bag, he had to walk over and comment. "Stocking up on snacks for the week?"

"What?" She stared at him. "I can afford my own snacks, Javier."

"Then what's this?"

Her cheeks reddened. "I was going to take it over to Corinna's Cupboard. When you make fresh food, it doesn't save well. Veronica and Alex and I got the idea together, yesterday when we were talking about quantities of food."

"You need to clear things like that with me."

"I'm sorry." She drew in a breath and then let it out slowly. "You're right. It's your restaurant. Is it okay if we donate the leftover food to Corinna's Cupboard instead of throwing it away?"

He blew out a breath. "Of course. I only meant—"

"Thanks," she interrupted. She turned away to finish bagging the food.

Leaving Javier feeling like a total jerk.

# CHAPTER SIX

AS SOON AS MOLLY reached the restaurant on Thursday morning, she saw Javier's car. *Just pretend he's a regular client and act normal,* she told herself.

Inside, she found Javier at the desk in the kitchen, going through paperwork.

"Excuse me," she said, "may I have a minute?"

"Of course." He scooted back and indicated the chair beside the desk. "What's up?"

She pulled out her tablet and made her smile neutral. "You'd asked me to run everything by you, so I brought in a draft of the new fresh menu we worked up. Would you like to check it?" She held the tablet out to him.

"Molly, I don't need—"

"It'll run parallel to the other menu, just a sheet inside. We can track the results and see how it goes."

"That's a good idea." He looked into her eyes as he handed back the tablet. "I trust your judgment on the food."

Yeah, right. Maybe he did, but that was the *only* area in which he trusted her. "That's great then. Thanks!" She stood quickly and turned away, hoping he wouldn't detect her complicated feelings toward him. Be a robot, she told herself. It was what she'd said often as a kid.

Her buzzing phone provided a welcome excuse to step further away. "Hello?"

"Mrs. Abbott?"

She wasn't a Mrs, but nobody needed to know that. "Yes?"

"This is Reba Henry at the middle school. If you have a moment, our principal, Mrs. Gooley, would like to speak with you."

"Is Trina okay?"

"The principal will be on the line in just a moment."

By the time Mrs. Gooley got on the phone, a couple of minutes later, Molly was pacing the kitchen of El Corazon, not even caring who saw her and asked questions. "Is Trina all right?" she asked immediately.

"Your daughter is fine. This isn't an emergency. But there's an issue I'd like to discuss with you."

"Today?" She'd planned to do all kinds of work this afternoon to get ready for the soft reopening, but she shrugged it aside in a moment.

"Today would be splendid. Eleven o'clock?"

"I'll be there." She clicked off the phone and im-

mediately kicked herself for not getting more information. What kind of an issue could Trina have that
was serious enough to involve the principal? Had she
done something wrong? Was she struggling in her
classes and concealing it from Molly?

She looked at her watch. It was 10:15 now, so
there was just enough time to finish a couple of things
here and then head for the school.

A schedule. She'd been working on a purchasing
schedule that would take advantage of produce from
two local farms. She bent over her notes.

But she couldn't concentrate. Instead, she chewed
her lip and worried about her daughter.

Javier approached her. "Is everything okay?"

"I don't know." She tapped her pencil on the table.
"The middle school principal called. She wants me to
come discuss some kind of issues with Trina."

"Do you know what it's about?"

She shook her head. She shouldn't confide in
Javier, but she didn't have anyone else to talk to, not
right now. "I'm worried. Trina's been up and down,
mood-wise, but I thought it was just typical preteen
emotions."

"Want me to drive you to the school?"

"No!" She stared at him. "I wouldn't ask that."

"But I'd offer it. Molly, whatever our differences, a
child is a child and more important than anything else.
It might be easier for you to collect yourself and help

Trina if someone else drives."

"I... " She should say no, be independent. But the truth was, her insides were in knots. She wiped her hands down the sides of her khakis. "That would be great. Thanks."

After asking a few questions Molly couldn't answer, Javier went silent and just drove, quickly, to the school. As soon as they were buzzed inside, he pointed her toward the office. "I'll be outside if you need me. Just text," he said.

Too worried to speak, she squeezed his hand and then spun toward the office. She signed in and sat down to wait, looking around at the bright turquoise walls, covered with posters. She tried to calm herself by reading each one: "You Matter!" and "The Hard Stuff Seems Impossible... Until You Do It" and "Success Starts with YOU." At the end of the front counter, a teacher leaned forward to talk with a secretary, their low voices indistinguishable.

A moment later, Principal Colette Gooley came out into the reception area, short and plump and grey-haired, with piercing black eyes. "Ah, Mrs. Abbott. I'm ready for you."

Molly followed her in, a bit intimidated by the woman's age and dignity. Although Molly had attended middle school here, she'd never been to the principal's office nor interacted with Dr. Gooley, who'd been new at the time.

As soon as they'd both sat down, Dr. Gooley behind the desk and Molly in front of it, the older woman got to the point. "Trina cut a class earlier today."

"She did?" Molly leaned forward, her mouth dry. Trina had always behaved well in school. "Is she all right? Did you find her?"

"Fortunately, another student reported that she was in the restroom crying. When our guidance counselor went to talk to her, she eventually admitted she'd been bullied by a couple of other girls."

Molly's heart plunged. "Oh, no! Where is she now?"

Dr. Gooley waved a hand. "She's in class. We don't allow teen or tween drama to interrupt education. But since Trina is new and the situation seemed serious, I wanted to discuss it with you."

Molly gripped the edge of her chair to keep from jumping up and hunting Trina down. "Did she tell you what happened?"

"Between her account and that of a couple of other young people it looks like a girl named Laura Jones was involved."

"Laura?" Involuntarily, Molly looked toward outer door that led to the parking lot. "But she's been a friend to Trina, and she seems like a lovely girl."

"Yes, indeed. However, she put a threatening note in Trina's locker and somehow, Trina was jostled, her books scattered on the floor. The halls are crowded and accidental bumps happen all the time, but Trina got very upset."

Molly squeezed her hands into fists. "Did she... Was Trina the one to tell you what happened?" If she had, that would mean Trina was totally devastated. Even last year when the bullying had gotten awful, she hadn't wanted to tattle.

"No. One of our sixth-graders, Maisie Felton, helped Trina pick up her things. When Trina wouldn't come report it, Maisie did." Dr. Gooley smiled. "Maisie's quite a strong defender of anyone in trouble. You wouldn't go wrong encouraging a friendship there."

"Thank you for letting me know." She drew in a breath and let it out in a sigh. "Any recommendations on what I should do?"

"I've already spoken to both girls, so the problem may be solved. But..." Dr. Gooley tapped a pencil on her desk and looked out the window into the school parking lot.

"I'll do anything to help my daughter."

"It's just... sometimes, a little intervention between parents can work better than heavy-handed school intervention, especially if we catch the problem at an early stage. Laura's mother is lovely, and if I recall correctly, you know her uncle as well."

Molly's head lifted at that, but Dr. Gooley was

blandly sorting through some paperwork. "It looks like Trina is a strong student. Getting her involved in a couple of extracurriculars wouldn't hurt. There's a musical, a service club, various athletic teams...."

"I'll do that."

Dr. Gooley stood. "Thank you for coming in so promptly. I'll leave you to take any initial steps you want to with Laura's family. If that's not effective and the problem continues, we'll take it from there. We don't look kindly on bullying here in Arcadia Valley."

When she went back out to the car, Javier came out to open the door for her. "Is Trina okay?"

"I'm not sure." Molly wished she had more time to think about it, but here was Laura's uncle—the very person she was supposed to talk to about the situation. Quickly, she told him what Dr. Gooley had said.

"Laura did that to Trina?" His brows drew together. "I can't believe it. She's been taught better."

"I didn't make it up, Javier."

"No, no, I didn't mean that. I just think there's more behind it. I'll talk to Mariana and we'll confront Laura. This won't happen again, Molly. I'll make sure of it."

His confidence about being able to control middle school behavior made her smile. Trust Javier. But the truth was, she did. In fact, as a person accustomed to being the helper, never the one helped, Javier's stern desire to intervene made her sag with relief. She'd have enough to deal with, with Trina, so it was good to know Javier would help take care of Laura.

Her phone buzzed and she looked down. Uncle Dale, so she clicked into the call. "Hey, Uncle Dale. Everything okay?"

"With me, yes. But your aunt is upset you haven't stopped by to see her."

Molly sighed. "I'm surprised she wants me to." But actually, she wasn't. If she and Trina had stopped by right away, Aunt Lisa would have said they were imposing on her. Since they hadn't, she felt neglected.

Molly didn't want to examine the reason for the nervous shame that tickled at her, that had kept her away from her aunt.

"I understand." His vagueness suggested that Aunt Lisa must be in the room. "She's fixed up a nice lunch, and she hopes you'll come join us."

"Now?"

"Yes. Please." There was an odd little emphasis on that "please."

"I'm out doing some things for Trina, but I can stop by in a little while. Would that be okay?" Her palms were sweating on the phone.

"Come now. Please?"

"Are you sure you're okay, Uncle Dale?"

But the phone clicked off.

JAVIER HEARD MOLLY'S INTAKE of breath and saw her hit a button on her phone. "What's wrong?"

"Nothing, I hope. Uncle Dale wants me to stop over." She texted something into her phone. "He's not answering. But he's not that good with cell phones." She bit her lip and her leg bounced up and down.

"You're worried about him."

"Yeah, it's just... the heart trouble. He doesn't need extra stress, and Aunt Lisa can be a little hard to deal with."

*She's so kind.* Her daughter, her uncle... she was a caretaker, and he liked that, because it was a value he shared. If it weren't for their history, they could be a great couple.

And where had *that* thought come from?

Automatically, Javier changed lanes and hit the turn signal to head toward Dale and Lisa's house.

"I don't... hey, you don't need to do that. Just take me back to the restaurant and I'll get my car."

"Let's just swing by now."

"That's not necessary." But her voice sounded uncertain.

"Sounds like it is."

She bit her lip and nodded. "Okay. Thank you. It's just... I haven't seen Aunt Lisa for a while. She's so unpredictable. I hate for you to have to deal with that."

He headed down her old street as memories flooded him. "We'll just say hi, and you can check on your uncle."

When he pulled into the driveway of Dale and Lisa's ranch-style house, he felt a surge of memories. How many times had he come here in Molly's high school years? First walking, then in a car. He remembered awkward dinners around their dining room table, attempts to hold hands without her aunt and uncle noticing. Truth was, he'd usually wanted to get her out from under their watchful eyes.

He glanced over at Molly to find her looking out the window, her head bent. Was she remembering the same things he was?

But she touched the cross around her neck. She was praying. For Uncle Dale? "I'll come around. He got out and went around to open her door.

Molly's aunt answered the door. She could have been a pretty woman, with her well-coifed hair and slender figure. But her tight frown gave her a sour look that made Javier want to avoid talking to her.

The tense set of Molly's shoulders suggested she felt the same.

The two women greeted each other and Molly hesitated, then hugged her aunt, who stood as rigid as a fencepost.

Things hadn't changed. Aunt Lisa had never seemed very affectionate, especially compared to Javier's own demonstrative family.

"It's about time you came to pay your respects," Lisa said. "From what Dale said, you were over here all the time before I got home. Practically settled in."

"How *is* Uncle Dale?" Molly looked past her aunt into the living room. "No, don't get up, I'll come there." She skirted her aunt and went to hug her uncle, who sat in a recliner in front of the television.

That left Javier to face Lisa Hooper, a woman he'd never been able to connect with and didn't much like. "I hope you had a good trip?" he asked when she didn't say anything.

"Oh, southern France is lovely in autumn. I could have stayed and stayed, but Dale has had all this on his plate." She looked toward the living room.

"I'm sorry to hear he's been in poor health."

"Yes, and to have Molly and that teenager descend on him…" She looked at him and shook her head.

Javier wasn't playing that game. "The three of them seemed to be enjoying each other's company when they came to El Corazon."

She sniffed. "You may as well come on in." She turned toward the kitchen and beckoned for him to follow her. "Would you like some tea?"

He glanced back at Molly before following. She was kneeling beside her uncle, holding his hand, listening to him talk. There was a smile on her face but her shoulders slumped a little.

She'd just had some bad news about her daughter

and she was in the midst of a difficult job at the restaurant. A job he wasn't making any easier. Yet she'd come rushing to the aid of her uncle, even at the expense of having to be in her unpleasant aunt's presence.

She'd always been a person who loved to serve others. He remembered how she used to insist on helping with the dishes at El Corazon, how she'd signed up for a club that matched kids with disabilities with other kids for social interaction. She'd even, as he recalled, made that the cool club to be in, and a lot of her friends had joined up.

But who was helping Molly?

He walked into the kitchen. "Tea would be nice," he said, "and I'm sure Molly would like some too."

Lisa lifted an eyebrow. "I'm surprised you're on such good terms with her after what she did to you."

Javier scooped sugar into his tea and focused on stirring it, even though he normally took it black.

"I don't know who spread the word about her... condition, back then, but everyone in town found out, and I felt terrible for you."

*Sure you did.* But her words scraped at a long-ago scar.

"Well. Of course, you're a good Christian. Seventy times seven, right?" She put a plate of vanilla sandwich cookies in front of him.

His mother had taught him not to refuse hospitality, so he took a cookie and bit into it. It tasted like dust in his mouth.

"How is dear Mariana?" Lisa asked.

Why was she asking... oh. "I forgot for a minute that you and Dale were friends with Petey. She's fine. Girls are getting big." And mean, if the bullying story was true.

Molly appeared in the doorway, her head cocked to one side as if she sensed some of the vibes in the room.

He stood, jostling the table in his haste. "Ready to go? Or if you'd like to stay, I can come back and pick you up later." Just as long as he got out of there now.

"I need to head back to work." She looked across the room at her aunt, who stood leaning back against the counter, arms crossed. "Aunt Lisa, I know you've got a lot on your hands with getting settled back in. If you'd like for me to take Uncle Dale to his doctor appointments, I'd be glad to."

*Smart,* Javier thought. *That way, you can see your uncle without her.*

"I can take my own husband to the doctor!"

*Except when you're busy touring Europe.*

"The offer's there," Molly said, her voice mild. "It's good to see you, Aunt Lisa. Maybe you can come to dinner soon, and see Trina."

Taking his plate and glass to the counter, Javier happened to glance at Lisa.

She was glaring at Molly, brows drawn together, posture rigid.

"She's a lovely girl. Twelve now." Molly's voice was still quiet, but she lifted her chin. "Again, the offer's open."

As they waved to Uncle Dale and left the house, Javier frowned. What a tense place to grow up or come home to. Poor Molly.

And yet... and yet.

How many people around town saw him and Molly and said to themselves what Lisa had said out loud? *I'm surprised you're on good terms with her after what she did to you.*

Yeah, he was a Christian. But not a perfect one.

# CHAPTER SEVEN

"D O THESE REFRIED BEANS taste okay without lard?" Molly held out a plate to Pablo. If it passed the older cook's test, it was a win.

"What's lard?" Trina asked.

"Pork fat, and if we leave it out, vegetarian customers can eat the beans."

"But you cannot make them without it." Pablo took a spoon and tasted the plate of beans, and his eyebrows rose. "Spicy! Chipotle?"

"And a little jalapeno. Is it too much? I used your recipe otherwise. Trina, taste these, will you?"

"No way!" Trina wrinkled her nose and backed away.

"*Delicioso*", Pablo said, "but we need to label them spicy. Some of our customers, especially the older Anglos, don't like that."

"Why are you so nervous, Mom?" Trina turned away from the counter, where she was pressing corn masa for tortillas, and looked severely at Molly. "It's what's inside you that counts, right? That's what you always tell me."

"You're pretty smart." Molly put an arm around her daughter. Thursday's incident at school had upset her and they'd talked about it, strategizing what to do if it happened again. But Friday had gone better because Trina had made friends with Maisie Felton, and they had plans to get together over the weekend. This morning, Trina had awakened in a fine mood and offered to come help at the restaurant for the big unveiling of Molly's new trial menu.

But with Trina settled, at least for now, Molly had only this important day to focus on, and she was a bundle of live nerves.

The door from the front of the restaurant opened, and Molly's heart rate accelerated. Was it Javier?

Nope. Laura walked in stiffly, holding a cake pan. She walked up to Trina. "I'm sorry I was mean. We made this for you."

*That* was a forced apology, for sure. Molly walked over to see the cake. Written on the top was, "Welcome to Arcadia Valley," in crooked script.

"That's really sweet, Laura," Molly said.

"Thanks," Trina said in a flat voice, taking the cake.

Both girls stood awkwardly, and Molly noticed that Laura's eyes were red. So maybe, in addition to being forced to apologize, she actually felt a little bit bad for what she'd done. "Hey Laura, could you help

Trina finish pressing the tortillas? I've got to check something out front." Maybe that would give them a chance to work out their differences, away from adults' interfering eyes.

Once she'd gone a few steps into the entryway that stretched between the two dining rooms, Molly heard Javier's deep voice coming from the left-hand room and stopped.

"I don't get it," Javier was saying. "Quintanas defend underdogs. You know that, right?"

A young girl's voice—Raquel's?—responded: "I know, Uncle Javier. You've told us a million times. Laura was trying to make friends with the wrong girls. She's sorry for it."

"Besides," came Mariana's voice, "it was you and your brothers and sister who defended underdogs. It wasn't that way for us. I *was* the underdog, and that's why I married Petey. He was strong." Her windy sigh corresponded with Molly's own sharp drawn-in breath. "But really... he was strong in a way that..." She paused.

"What, Mama?" Raquel asked.

"Never mind. Your father was a confident, charming man who loved you girls very much."

"That's the truth," Javier chimed in. "He was very successful, and the life of the party, but he knew his family was the important thing."

Molly sank into a chair in the entryway, arms

clasped around her middle. The words she'd over-heard made her insides roil. Partly, because she couldn't tell the truth about Trina's parentage without destroying a local hero to his own daughters. But partly because the words made her remember what had made her vulnerable to Petey.

He *had* been a good-looking, popular, life of the party type of man, loud and funny. Everyone had loved him.

When he'd started to pay extra attention to Molly, God forgive her, she'd liked it. She hadn't felt that special since her parents died, and she'd eagerly accepted his gifts and invitations.

To her, Petey had been the father she'd lost. She hadn't intended to lead him on. But despite all her counseling, she still felt a slick sense of shame when she remembered the names Aunt Lisa had called her when Molly had gone to her, telling her about the assault.

It was like Petey had said. No one believed her. Maybe she *had* done something to provoke the attack, however innocently.

Her stomach churned.

She shook the memories and the bad feelings out of her head and hurried over to the CD player. To go along with the new trial menu, she'd brought a CD of a contemporary Mexican singer-songwriter, and now she set it to playing, softly.

Only then did she dare to glance into the dining room. Mariana and Raquel sat at a table, sipping coffee, while Javier wiped a speck from the window.

Veronica came in from the back, taking off her sweater. "It's go time," she said. "Abuela and her friends are here."

Mariana laughed. "The real judges."

In the front door came four women, talking rapidly, all upwards of seventy. One used a three-footed cane, and another had distinctly blue-grey hair. The leader of the pack had dyed-red hair and a flamboyant pink and yellow caftan. And there was Javier's grandmother, dressed in dark, conservative clothes, and still the prettiest of the group.

Javier hurried over, kissed his grandmother and all the other ladies, and then escorted them to a table. Soon they studied the menu and chatted, glancing around. Was it her imagination, or were they talking about her?

Other people came into the restaurant now, no doubt attracted by the new sign, the offered deals, and word of mouth. Molly's heart seemed to flutter in her throat. She'd consulted with restaurants before and it had been exciting, but this was different, personal.

She looked at the portrait of Javier's parents. What great people. His mother had been way more motherly than Aunt Lisa had been, and Molly had loved her dearly.

As Veronica took the first set of orders back to the kitchen, Javier said under his breath, "here goes nothing."

"I wish you weren't so worried." Molly walked to the kitchen with him.

"When my family's reputation is on the line, I take it seriously." He held the swinging door open for her.

Of course he did. It was one of the things she admired about him, his devotion to duty and family.

She looked through and saw Trina and Laura by the open back door, talking intently. "When my livelihood and my daughter's happiness are on the line, I take it seriously, too," she said. Her arm brushed his, and every nerve felt the connection.

Their eyes met and held. His face, the square jaw and dark handsomeness, had been so dear to her in the past. But she couldn't be thinking about that at this important professional time.

She turned away from him and toward the cooks—Pablo had been joined by Maria—and inhaled the scent of cilantro and onions. "How is it to cook the new recipes?" she asked.

Pablo nodded. "Interesting."

But Maria shook her head. "A lot of the Anglos don't want this real Mexican stuff. They want crispy tacos and deep-fried chimichangas."

"Chain restaurant stuff? Are those our target customers?"

Maria gestured toward the front of the restaurant, where a waiter was carrying out the first plates of food. "When they're Abuela's friends, yes."

Uneasiness wrapped tentacles around Molly's stomach. Would this work? Would Javier be happy? She really, really wanted him to be happy.

"Need a hand putting together these tacos," Pablo called, and Molly gestured to Trina.

"I can help, too," Laura said.

"Come on, then, put gloves on."

Whew. The rift between the girls seemed to be solved.

"Molly, c'mere!" Veronica gestured from the doorway to the front. "They're tasting the food!"

Molly went over feeling sick and hopeful at the same time.

Abuela said something they couldn't hear, her forehead wrinkling. Then they all looked toward the lady in the colorful caftan.

She beckoned to Javier, who'd been ushering a group to a table, and swallowed her bite of food. "Javier," she said, "your mother would turn over in her grave if she tasted this."

Abuela and the other women answered and a quiet argument broke out, but Molly had had enough. Her stomach knotted and she collapsed into a chair in the hallway. She'd seen Javier's face fall, and Veronica looked worried.

The worst had happened. The new plan was a disaster.

TWO DAYS LATER, Javier looked across the table at Molly and felt the incredible mix of feelings that she always evoked in him. Nostalgia, attraction, frustration, and anger simmered inside him.

The buzz of *Mexico Nuevo,* a popular Twin Falls restaurant, would normally have kept his attention, but he couldn't seem to focus on anything but her.

She looked up from her note pad and raised her eyebrows. "What?"

He couldn't explain it, not really. "Did you get good ideas from here?" he asked instead.

"I think so." She chewed on the end of her pencil. "I see how they do things traditional Mexican, but with a twist of new. I think I went too far in the trendy direction with that menu. We need to offer more old-style options."

"Coming here was a good idea," he said. "I like that you're sensitive to what El Corazon needs."

"I was mortified that your grandma didn't like the food."

"I talked to her. She didn't hate it, she was just kind of reserving judgment. It was Loretta who didn't like it. The trouble is, she's spreading the word, which makes my grandma look bad."

"I'm so sorry, Javier. I didn't mean to cause you

embarrassment or stress. That's the last thing I'm supposed to do."

The waiter brought the check and she reached for it. He pulled it out from under her hand. "I'll get this."

"No, Javier, this is a work thing. I'll write it off."

Indignation sliced through him. Was that what she'd thought, that their dinner at a rival restaurant was all about work?

Which, of course, it was. But still. "I'll get it," he said. "I don't like letting a woman pay."

She blew out a breath. "What century is it again? I'm a successful business owner."

"And I'm a traditional gentleman." He pulled out his wallet.

She shook her head, and then she smiled, reached over, and gave his arm a brief little rub. "I know, you've always been like that and you probably aren't going to change. So thank you for dinner. I appreciate it."

With that little touch, and what it did to his heart rate, she completely belied the notion that this was a work-only outing.

After he'd paid, they walked slowly through the restaurant, observing everything. They'd already talked to the manager, but now the bartender called them over. "Hey," he said, "remember me? Quinto Rodriguez."

"Hey!" Javier shook the man's hand. "This is Molly Abbott. A year behind us in school."

"I remember," Quinto said, looking Molly up and down. "Everyone does."

Javier put an arm around Molly, wanting instinctively to protect her from a random man's gawking. At the same time, he felt the nick to his pride. Everyone in town remembered their past, what she'd done to him, and now, it looked like everyone out of town did too.

He looked at Molly's face. She'd lifted her chin and was giving Quinto a level stare, but from Javier's vantage point, he saw the muscle twitching in her cheek. "Did you have a question about something?" she asked.

"No. No." Quinta focused on the glasses he was drying and putting away. "You folks have a nice evening."

As they turned away, Molly blew out a slow, controlled breath. And Javier realized she'd probably had to deal with similar questions ever since high school.

No wonder she'd stayed away from Idaho. The reactions to her pregnancy out of wedlock seemed especially severe here, and he wasn't sure why. Just a conservative area, he supposed. Or the fact that the boyfriend she'd cheated on had been a Quintana. For better or worse, their family had always been a lot in the public eye, due to the restaurant and to Alex's stint in Major League Baseball.

In the face of what she had to put up with each day, his own self-pity seemed minor. He fiercely wanted to protect her from rumors and innuendos, from any kind of pain.

He led the way out and then turned to make sure she got down the stairs okay. As he held out a hand to help her, realization swept over him.

Despite his mixed feelings and leftover anger, he was in love with her. Still. Maybe he'd never stopped being in love with her.

It seemed natural to keep hold of her hand as they walked to the parking lot. Natural to hold the door for her.

And when they headed out of Twin Falls, it seemed natural to take the turnoff to Centennial Waterfront Park. "Take a look?" he invited. "Will Trina be okay?"

"I hope so. I was surprised Aunt Lisa offered to stay with her, but they were shopping online when I left and having a pretty good time. Maybe Aunt Lisa is growing a heart."

They strolled to the picnic area and sat down on a bench, looking out at trees and blue sky and sunlight reflected in the water below, smelling the pungent sage.

"I love Idaho," she said, sighing. "Ohio was nice, but cornfields can't compare to this view."

"I'm glad you came home."

"I'm pretty sure I am, too."

They both leaned back. Molly lifted her face to the breeze. He could feel her warmth a fraction of an inch from his arm.

Off to the side of the picnic area, he saw the trail that branched off toward the water. Memory surfaced with the force of a geyser. It was where they'd first kissed. Had he subconsciously parked here on purpose, to call up the old days?

He glanced over at her, and something in the pink of her cheeks made her think that she remembered, too.

Before he could think better of it, he spoke. "Do you want to walk by the river? For old times' sake?"

She studied him for a minute, biting her very pretty lip. "We did have fun together, didn't we?"

He nodded. "It was the best."

"This is just... for old times' sake?" The skin between her eyebrows crinkled.

He crooked his arm for her to grab onto. "That's right. Come on."

She took his arm, her small fingers curling around his bicep.

As he led the way to the boat docks at the river's edge, every inch of his skin seemed alive to her nearness.

They walked in silence for a moment, looking at

the high rock walls and the flowing water, and listening to the cheeps and chatters of ground squirrels. It was pure, it was clean, and it compelled honesty. What secrets could withstand God's natural beauty?

He glanced over to find her looking at him.

"What are you thinking about?" she asked.

"Molly, why did you…" He broke off. "I'm sorry. I'm trying my best to let the past go. It's a new day."

"That's how it has to be." She held a little tighter to his arm.

She'd used to cling to his arm when they were dating, and now her touch was the same… but not. She'd grown up into a stunning, confident woman, and her grasp on his arm reflected that.

And she was even more intoxicating than she'd been as a girl.

He tried to focus on the fresh tang of sage, on the sound of the water against the dock. But he couldn't stop his thoughts and feelings from racing ahead.

Could he and Molly be together again? Was there a chance for them? But there wasn't if she was keeping a secret, was there?

"Is there a good reason why you can't tell me about Trina's father?"

She looked up at him and blew out a sigh. "Yes, Javier, there is."

"Do you still have a connection with him?"

She shook her head. "No. I don't."

He nodded and they walked on. Their relationship had been shallow and immature in high school. He saw that now. It had held an innocence, too, that had been beautiful in the way that any true first love was beautiful.

They could never have that relationship again. They were different people.

But maybe they could keep some of the old, and build something new as well. Maybe some amount of change could be good. Maybe the present could be a mixture, of past traditions plus new, exciting things.

He hopped off the dock to stand on the river's edge, and held out a hand for her to do the same. She hesitated, just as she had back then. Probably nervous, again, at following him into a more secluded area of the park.

"Come on," he encouraged her. When she didn't move, he added, "I want to ask you something."

She bit her lip, then took his hand and hopped down, dropping it immediately.

He took a rock and skipped it, just as he'd done the day of their first kiss. "Did you ever learn to skip rocks?" he asked.

"That's what you wanted to ask me?"

He smiled at her, nodded.

She shook her head. "I never tried with anyone but you."

He swallowed, bent down, and picked up a handful of flat rocks. Then he took her arm and stood behind her. "First," he said, "you pull back your arm like this." He wrapped his arm around hers, pulling hers across her chest and back to the side. Which brought them so close together that he could smell her rose scent and feel her warmth.

"So what... do I do... next?"

"Next," he said, "you bend your wrist like so." He bent her small wrist to give her leverage. "Got the position?"

"I think so." Her voice sounded breathless.

He stepped away. "And then," he demonstrated, "you flip it out over the water." He did, and his rock skipped four, five times.

She did the same, and hers sank.

"I'm terrible at this!"

"You need practice. Here." He put another rock in her hand. "Remember, it's all in the flip of the wrist."

She bit her lip, watched him demonstrate again, and then flicked her own rock out. Again it sank. But she squatted down and picked up more rocks, and flicked them out, over and over, until finally, she got a rock to skip a couple of times.

She wouldn't have been that persistent in past times. She'd gotten stronger.

She squatted again, selected a flat rock, stood, and flipped it out across the water. It skipped three times before splashing in.

"I did it!" She turned to him, cheeks pink, eyes sparkling, and she was quite simply the most beautiful, compelling woman he'd ever seen.

Yeah, she'd done something to him that he still couldn't completely forgive. And she still wasn't being completely honest with him.

It wouldn't be wise at all to start things up with her.

She lifted her chin and smiled at him. "I bet I can beat you at skipping."

Drawn to her like a magnet, he reached for her, but she stepped back, laughing, and bent to pick up a handful of rocks. Expert now, she flipped rock after rock onto the water, making most of them skip and skip again.

"See?" she said triumphantly.

This time, he reached for her faster, gripped her forearms before she could dart away. "I see, all right," he murmured, pulling her just a little closer. "I see a beautiful woman who can still play like a girl." He moved a little closer.

Her eyes widened.

He touched her chin and let his hand slide along her jawline until it tangled in her hair.

She drew in her breath with a little gasp.

So she did still feel something for him, still responded to his touch. With an inner groan, he lowered his lips to hers.

# CHAPTER EIGHT

KISSING JAVIER WASN'T at all like she remembered from years ago.

Then, he'd been a little hesitant, unsure of his reception or maybe just inexperienced. Not now.

His lips moved gently on hers, and she felt it all the way to her toes, involuntarily standing on tiptoe in an effort to get closer. He tugged her against his chest, and deepened the kiss.

She put up her hands to push him away a little, but couldn't make herself do it.

Finally, overwhelmed by her own intense feelings, she pulled back, and he gazed at her, a question in his eyes.

She inhaled the river's moist perfume. She couldn't speak, not really.

"I'm sorry about my beard."

She reached up to stroke his stubble. "It's heavier than it was in high school."

"Did it hurt?"

She shook her head.

"Good. I never want to hurt you." He touched her face gently.

Was this Javier, who'd once been so angry with her, being tender? She looked into his eyes, and he held her gaze, communicating without words.

Above them, an eagle soared, sun flashing on its golden feathers. Its powerful beak and talons were visible as it swooped down toward the earth.

She heard its hoarse *wip-wip* call, and a shiver ran over her.

Javier pulled her to him and kissed her forehead, her hair. Her hands rested against his chest and she couldn't help the smile that curved her mouth, the excitement speeding up her heart rate.

"Oh, Molly. My Molly," he murmured, just as he had so many years ago. "What's going to come of this? I'm starting to think we may have something together."

Yes. But it scared her. "We should get back." She doubted Trina and Aunt Lisa would get along for hours on end.

They walked back to the car, not talking, holding hands. The world around them was a pleasant haze.

Something sparkled on the path and she bent down to pick it up. She held up the shiny gold rock to Javier. "Look! I always heard there was gold along the Snake River!"

He chuckled, taking the rock and holding it to the

fading light. "That's pyrite. Fool's gold." He held it back out to her. "Want to keep it? For old time's sake?"

She met his eyes and took the rock from him, folding it into her free hand.

The farther they got from the river, the more thoughts invaded her happy haze. She was trying to build a life here in Arcadia Valley, for herself but most of all, for Trina. But they couldn't go forward without him knowing the truth about Trina's conception, and how would he take it? With compassion, or with disbelief and judgment?

And what if she failed with El Corazon? That was the whole reason they were even out tonight. His family's restaurant was everything to him. Maybe he was just being kind to her while the restaurant fix was happening. It hardly seemed possible that he liked her for herself.

He held the door for her, and once she got in, he leaned down and touched her chin. "Hey. Don't overthink this."

"Okay." But what did *that* mean? That she shouldn't take it seriously?

If she got close to Javier and then he rejected her, she'd have to leave Arcadia Valley. She couldn't withstand being here and watching him fall in love with someone else, get married, have children. Not if she'd let her heart get involved.

She needed to stop this in its tracks.

He pulled out of the parking lot and then reached over and took her hand, squeezed it.

The breath wooshed from her lungs.

There was nothing she wanted more than to restart her relationship with Javier.

There was nothing that would be a bigger mistake.

Back at the cottages, he came around and opened her door for her. When she got out, he closed the door and started up the little walkway toward the cottage.

"You don't have to walk me to the door, Javier. It wasn't a date."

"Wasn't it?" He lifted an eyebrow.

"No, it wasn't." She tried to make her voice firm, without success.

"A gentleman doesn't let a lady go home alone." He softened the old-fashioned words with a smile. "What if a monster were hiding in the bushes beside the door, ready to jump out and eat you?"

A chill ran over her.

He put an arm around her. "You forgot how cold Idaho gets at night. Here." He wrapped his own jacket around her.

"You don't need to... Thank you," she said.

The moment they reached the door, it opened. "It's about time you got back—oh." Aunt Lisa looked at Javier, and then back at Molly, wearing his jacket. "Really? Even after... everything?"

As usual, her aunt had a way of battering down Molly's confidence. Why had she agreed to have Aunt Lisa babysit Trina? But then again, there'd been no one else, and twelve wasn't really old enough to stay alone for more than a short time.

"I'm going to get my things and go." Aunt Lisa walked over to the couch, grabbed her purse, and pushed past them.

"Wait. I really appreciate your staying with Trina. How'd it go?"

"That girl is the rudest thing I've ever seen, and she's likely to grow up just like you."

A giant rock formed in Molly's stomach. "What happened?"

"I'm sure she'll tell you, but take it with a grain of salt. She lies, just like you always did." She stalked out toward her car.

Her aunt's words cut deep, even though Molly knew the source wasn't an accurate one. She stepped inside and looked back at Javier. "Thank you—"

Trina came out of her bedroom, pushing the door hard enough that it slammed back against the wall, and stood, hands on hips. Her eyes were red and swollen. "Mom! Is it true?"

"What, honey?" Molly's heart thumped hard, then skittered a rapid drumbeat. She hurried to her daughter.

"Is it true that Aunt Lisa knows who my father

is?"

JAVIER STALKED ACROSS the yards to his own cottage, his thoughts in turmoil. He'd already been reeling from kissing Molly. Now, to hear that her aunt knew who Trina's father was? Which, apparently, was more than Trina herself knew?

Instinctively, he'd offered to help when Trina's turmoil became apparent, but Molly had waved him away. Of course, it was a mother-daughter conversation and he shouldn't interfere.

Besides, if he were there, he might learn the secret she didn't want him to know.

He roamed around his cottage for a couple of minutes, but he couldn't calm down. He needed to do something physical.

His garden. Or so-called garden, because it wasn't much. He needed to turn over the earth and mulch it for winter. But that particular task never rose to the top of the priority list.

No time like the present. He stalked out to the common gardens and was ashamed to see how his own overgrown plot compared with other residents' neat rows.

He grabbed a big shovel from the common tool-shed and went to work.

He pulled out giant weeds and overgrown squash vines. Funny how the weeds and good plants mixed all together, to the point where you couldn't disentangle them. This garden was long gone.

Wasn't there a bible verse about that? A master told his servants not to pull the weeds out of a garden, but to let them grow with the main plants and they'd be separated out later?

He dug, pulled. Sweat popped out on his body as his muscles strained. Soon, he had a stack of weeds and plants to compost and dark earth brought to the top. The smell of it rose to his nostrils, calming him.

Molly was a good person in a lot of ways: a loving mother, a hard worker, tender and sweet. But there were some weeds in her too, weeds of deceit and betrayal.

Uneasiness nudged at him as he considered that he had his own weedy parts. He was a sinner like anyone else. His sins just tended toward perfectionism and judgment of others.

Still, he wasn't going to let himself get caught up in Molly's garden again, delightful as it might be. He'd wait and see how it all turned out.

A light flipped on at Molly's house and she walked out onto the porch, alone. Stood leaning forward on the railing, looking up at the stars. Her shoulders were slumped.

If he were a good friend, he'd go to her. Help her out. But they'd already gotten too close today.

He ducked his head and continued to dig, breaking

up the dirt.

TWO DAYS AFTER the disastrous episode between Trina and Aunt Lisa, Molly was still reeling as she worked at a table in El Corazon, finalizing plans for the soft reopening next week. The restaurant was quiet in the morning before anyone else had come in, and sometimes, she found she was able to think and ponder better being in the space alone.

Worries about Trina kept sidetracking her from her lists and phone calls. Molly and Trina had talked, and Molly had explained that hearing more details about her father was going to be hard. Whenever Trina was ready, though, she could hear the truth.

Fortunately—at least, Molly thought it was fortunate—Trina had backed away from the story, mumbling that she had too much homework to talk about it that night.

In other words, she wasn't ready to hear it just now.

But Trina's issues about her father were going to come to the forefront. So far in Trina's childhood, Molly had followed the recommendations of two counselors she'd consulted and had only answered the questions Trina had asked. She'd told Trina the truth—"your father had serious problems that made him do unkind things, and so we don't talk to him"— but had kept it purposely vague.

Now, since Lisa had pushed the issue, Trina was back to wondering. The time would come, maybe soon, when Molly would have to reveal the whole ugly story. It was complicated by the fact that Molly's best friends were actually her half-sisters. The stuff of soap operas, but not nearly so entertaining.

She had an appointment with a counselor here to help her figure out the new normal, and she planned to consult Pastor Harris from Arcadia Valley Community Church, now their church home.

For the moment, Trina was avoiding the issue and had rebuffed a couple of Molly's attempts to talk about it—more proof that she wasn't ready to deal with the answers. Which was fine, as long as they stayed away from Aunt Lisa.

Her phone buzzed. "Molly? It's Maria. I can't get ahold of Pablo or Javier. I'm really sorry, but I need to call off tonight."

"Sure, I can leave a note or let one of them know when they come in. I'll be here, and I can help out. Is everything okay?"

"I'm fine, and I feel awful about missing. I was supposed to do the prep work this morning. But my mother is sick and can't take care of Tomasito, and I haven't been able to find anyone else. To top it off, my car's in the shop."

"Do you... can I help?" Molly asked. "I could come and get you, bring you both back to the restaurant I can keep an eye on Tomasito."

"That's too much to ask. You have your work to do."

"I love babies. And my work is flexible."

"Well..."

"You're a lot better at prep work than I am. Really, it's no problem."

"Could you? Oh, Molly, that would be wonderful. I'd really appreciate it." Quickly, she gave Molly directions to her house, and after tying up a few loose ends, Molly headed there.

The frame house was modest, with a small front yard, but Molly glimpsed what looked like a substantial garden out behind. "Is that corn you have growing?"

Maria nodded, hitching her sleepy one-year-old higher on her hip. "Four varieties. Come on, you can see out the back window."

As they walked through the kitchen, Molly looked around and stopped. The several hanging bunches of chili peppers were no surprise, but Maria also had glass jars of beans and quinoa and what looked like pumpkin seeds. A large cloth bag held *masa harina*, the corn flour used to make tortillas. A cast iron tortilla press and two mortars and pestles stood ready on the counter, and there was a colander of fresh greens in the sink. "This is a great kitchen." She pointed to the greens. "Lambsquarters?"

"Mom calls them *quelites*. We gather them ourselves, when... when she's able." Maria's face went sad for a moment.

Molly reached out to tickle the baby's chin. "Hey, Tomasito, you going to hang out with me a little bit today?"

The baby chortled, then hid his face.

"Our garden gets bigger every year," Maria said. "We grow most of what we need, honestly."

Molly looked out on the neat rows of corn, squash, beans, and peppers. "Do you do any canning?"

"We can, and dry, and freeze. We enjoy it and it's healthier." She gathered her purse and keys. "Thanks so much for coming to get me."

"I'm happy to do it. And to know more about your expertise. Do Javier and Pablo realize what a gem they've got in you?"

Maria grabbed a car seat from beside the front door. "I've only been working there a year, and I feel lucky to have the job. Javier's a great boss."

"Well, but it must have been killing you to open cans of refried beans and jars of salsa."

Maria nodded. "I'm definitely glad to see the changes you're making."

"With your help, and Pablo's." Molly strapped the car seat into the back of her vehicle.

"Seems like Javier likes you." Maria said the

words quietly.

"Sometimes, sometimes not." Molly sighed as they started back toward the restaurant. "If I had time for a boyfriend, the rollercoaster might bother me, but I don't. Work and Trina keep me busy."

Maria snapped her fingers. "You should come to our Busy Women's Bible Study! We meet once a month at my house, more often if somebody has a problem and needs prayer. Veronica comes sometimes, and Gloria Sinclair. Also Kate Groves, who runs the farmers' market, and Charlotte MacGregor, when she can get away from the library."

"Are you open to new members?" Molly asked, feeling wistful. "Sometimes those kind of groups like to keep membership small."

"Not us." Maria continued to tick off members on her fingers. "My mom comes when she's feeling good. So does her friend Irene Turner, who owns the bookstore. Not everyone comes every time, and we don't allow guilt about missing. But it's a great group, so everyone comes as often as they can."

"I would love that. I need woman friends." And as they pulled back into El Corazon's parking lot, Molly felt heartened. Like she had an ally, about the changes she was trying to make at El Corazon, and maybe, soon, a spiritual ally as well.

# CHAPTER NINE

LATER THAT AFTERNOON, Molly sat on her front porch. The sun slanted more than it had weeks ago, indicating that autumn was near, but the air was still plenty warm. In her hands was a new menu for the soft reopening at El Corazon, and she loved what they'd done with it. This time, working with Maria and Pablo and even consulting with Javier's grandmother, she was pretty sure she'd found the right mix of tradition and innovation.

She ought to be happy. But she was waiting for Trina to come home on the bus, and Trina was still moody since the talk with Aunt Lisa. And Javier had promised to stop by and go over the menu with her. She didn't know whether to expect a warmhearted lover or a cold, distant client.

A breeze kicked up, bringing with it a few golden aspen leaves. In the ponderosa pine out front, a magpie scolded.

Next door, a bang and clatter indicated Javier coming down the steps. So he was going to be her first challenge.

*Give me strength, Lord.*

He came up her steps briskly. "You have a menu for me to look at?"

Okay. Businesslike client, then. "Yes, it's right here. Would you like to go inside so we can sit at a table?"

"No, this is fine." He sat down and held out his hand.

She passed the menu over to him. "I actually have one of the items for you to try, if you'd like."

"All right." He perused the menu. "Hmm. This is different from the one you did before."

"That's kind of the point. I hadn't been thinking about how many choices people were used to at El Corazon, so this version has a lot more variety."

"Including some of our old dishes."

"Uh-huh. Do you think I chose the right ones? I talked to Pablo about which were the most popular."

"Gringo-style Tacos?"

"You know, the ones with the crispy shells."

"I know what they are, I just question calling them that. We tend to emphasize unity, not division, and we have both Latino and non-Latino customers. Some might get offended."

"Okay, what should I call them?"

He grinned. "Terrible Tacos? Because they *are* pretty terrible."

Her breath caught. There was the fun-loving side of Javier, and she wanted him to stay that way with an ache that settled in her heart.

"Kidding. How about Crispy Tacos?"

"Perfect," she said, writing it down on her note pad.

He approved the avocado, potato, and chorizo tacos and the tamales with pork and a jicama-green-chili side salad, but drew the line at the duck carnitas. "That'll take a lot of time and expense, and knowing Arcadia Valley, there won't be much of a market for it."

"Don't be too sure." But she'd expected to lose some battles, so she made a note to delete that item from the final menu. "I also think you should give Maria a raise and more say in what goes on in the kitchen."

"Maria's new!"

"She's been here for a year." Molly explained what she'd seen at Maria's house. "She knows a lot about sustainability and using food for health. She's a great resource."

"Something to think about," he admitted.

"Hey, guys!" Mariana grinned as she approached with Cowboy on a leash. "Nice day, huh?"

"Sure is." As always, Molly felt a little uncomfortable seeing Mariana, but she genuinely liked the older woman. Now, she had a brainstorm. "Would you like to try a snack? I'm experimenting with something for the restaurant, and I need more than just Javier's input."

"Hey, are you saying I'm biased?" he protested.

"Old fashioned," Molly said.

"Totally," Mariana agreed, climbing the steps and sitting down on the top one, leaning back against a post to soak up the sun.

As Molly warmed up tortillas, she heard the low rumble of their voices outside and resolved to get over her mixed feelings about Mariana. The past was the past. She and Trina were blessed to be a part of this neighborhood and this community. If only they could stay here.

She buttered and salted the tortillas and rolled them up, then took them to the porch in a napkin-covered basket. "Here you go, amped up afternoon snack."

She held out the basket to Mariana, then to Javier, and they each looked curiously at them and then tasted.

"I did a little digging with your brothers and sister," Molly confessed, wanting to fill up the silent air and give them a chance to form an opinion. "I heard this is how your mom fixed tortillas for you guys, but these are a little different. I'm calling them amped up tortillas or fusion tortillas, you can help me decide which."

"They're good!" Mariana was the first to speak. "What's in them?"

"Flax and chia seeds and a little coarse-ground cornmeal, in addition to the regular masa harina. Otherwise, they're just pressed and cooked like regular corn tortillas."

They both looked at Javier, who was chewing and frowning.

Molly's heart sank.

Then he swallowed and smiled. "Almost as good as Mama's," he admitted, "and I haven't said that about any tortillas since she passed on."

Joy filled Molly's heart, too much joy for such a simple comment.

The school bus chugged to a stop, and a moment later, Trina and Laura got off the bus and headed toward the cottage. "See ya," Trina said to Laura in a cool voice. She came up the steps and inside with only a wave to the adults.

"Is she okay?" Mariana asked Laura, who'd followed along more slowly.

Laura rolled her eyes. "She's being silly because Terrance McKinley gave her his jacket."

"Terrance McKinley? Isn't he a ninth grader?"

"Tenth," Trina said from inside the screen door, her voice triumphant.

"Come back out a minute," Molly ordered, and Trina seemed all too happy to comply. Sure enough, she was dressed in a football letterman's jacket over her casual top and capris.

"That's too expensive of a gift," Molly said. "He must have been loaning it to you, right? Did something happen?"

"No, he just gave it to me because he likes me." Trina didn't look at Molly.

"All the other girls are jealous," Laura contributed. "Terrance is… " she glanced at her mother. "He's cute. Though not always very nice."

"I want you to give it back," Molly said. "Tell him you appreciate it, but your mother won't let you accept gifts from boys."

"Mom!"

Molly held up a hand. "I mean it. You give it back tomorrow, or if you don't want to, I'll take it to school and have the office give it back to him. There's no good reason for a tenth grade boy to give a seventh-grade girl his expensive jacket as a gift."

"You don't really want me to fit in here! You won't even tell me the truth about…" She looked around, pressed her lips together, and ran into the house.

Mariana stood. "Come on, Laura. Sounds like they need to work this out without an audience."

Javier stood too. "Are you okay?" He put a hand on Molly's shoulder.

"I hate you! You're a terrible mother!" came from

the other side of the screen door.

For just a moment, Molly leaned into Javier. This whole situation was proving damaging to Trina in ways she hadn't anticipated. Now, Trina was getting attention from a much older boy, attention she didn't know how to handle.

Molly straightened, blinked the tears from her eyes, and took a fortifying breath. This was what it was like being a single parent. You dealt with things alone. With God's help, but essentially alone.

"We'll be fine. Let me know if you want any other changes to the menu, and we'll talk tomorrow."

For tonight, she was going to try to undo the damage to her little girl.

THE NEXT SUNDAY, Javier pulled into the parking area at Bigby Farm practically right behind Molly and Trina.

His brother Daniel, riding shotgun, looked over at him. "Isn't that Molly and her daughter? We could've given them a ride."

"Or not." Javier gestured back toward Daniel's twins. "They'd have been crowded with two car seats."

Besides, he'd been trying to keep a little distance. Of course, coming to a picnic sponsored by the church Molly and Trina attended was no way to do that. He'd been relieved to learn that they were attending

Arcadia Valley Community Church rather than Grace Fellowship where most of the Quintanas went, but in truth, there was more cooperation than rivalry between the town's two evangelical churches. Javier and his brother Daniel had started coming to the AVCC picnic right after high school, supposedly to publicize El Corazon, but really to look at all the pretty girls. They'd never stopped doing either thing.

In fact, come to think of it, Daniel had forced him into coming after Molly had left town, trying to get him to date other people. Which he'd done. Occasionally.

No one had ever made his blood race the way Molly did, even now, as she climbed out of her car in a plaid shirt and old jeans, hair in a ponytail.

"This is dumb," he heard Trina say defiantly, and then came Molly's murmuring voice. Molly was having a time of it with her daughter. He'd heard a fair amount of shouting and door slamming over at their cottage in the past few days.

Daniel looked over at the pair and shook his head. "I am *not* looking forward to when the twins hit puberty."

"What's poob-tee, Daddy?" came from the back seat.

Javier laughed. "You brought it up, Dad."

Daniel murmured some kind of explanation as he helped Kaylee out of her car seat, while Javier helped little Haylee. Not so little anymore. She could climb to the ground perfectly well by herself. Amazing it had been three-and-a-half years since they'd been born. Three years since their mother had died.

"Look, Uncle Javie, goats!"

"Can we go see them, Daddy, please?"

"Wait for me." Daniel turned to Javier. "Can you manage the food?"

"Go. See you around."

He drew in a breath of farm fresh air as he opened up the car's trunk to pull out the food trays. He could still see Molly and Trina by their car, but they weren't arguing anymore. Nobody, not even a sulky twelve year old, could remain miserable at Bigby Farm.

He gazed around, appreciative of the big old barn, with fields of lavender beyond, and the homey looking farmhouse surrounded by a porch. An enclosure held goats who seemed unimpressed by the surrounding kids' shrieks. Caroline Hearst and her grandmother and cousins had done wonders with this place.

He started toward the food tables where clusters of people were gathering, which took him directly past Molly and Trina. Molly's face lit up a little before she frowned. "I thought the Quintanas went to Grace Fellowship?"

"Arcadia Valley Community Church opens the picnic to anyone who wants to come, so a lot of people in town do. It's a chance to hang out at Bigby

Farm, and show off your cooking abilities at the same time. What's not to like?"

"What did you bring?" she asked.

"Enchiladas from the restaurant. It's a tradition, and good PR."

Her eyes lit up. "That's something we can totally use in the redo!"

"Yes, but—" He held the pan away from her, grinning "–these are *traditional* enchiladas. Way too old fashioned for you."

"Oh, Javier." She shook her head, laughing a little. "That's okay. They're one of your best items. They're still on the revised menu."

He looked at the pie plate in her hands. "What did you bring?"

"Aunt Lisa's apple pie. It's kind of a peace offering. Showing she had a positive influence on me as I grew up, because one of the good things she did for me was teach me to cook."

"I don't see why you're trying to get along with her, Mom." Trina stalked along beside them. "She's mean."

"She's family. We do our best to get along with family."

Javier nodded. He wholeheartedly agreed.

But he also saw what Trina meant. Lisa wasn't up to any good, and rumor had it her gossip and mean behavior had gotten worse lately, possibly connected to her overusing pain pills. That could explain her erratic behavior, and it also meant she needed help before getting close to a vulnerable kid like Trina. Or Molly, either, for that matter.

When they got to the main crowd of people, several church members approached to greet Molly and Trina, including a girl who knew Trina from math class and suggested she come over and help with the little kids. Trina sighed, then smiled. "Sure, if you need me."

"Good." Molly watched the two girls walk away. "I want her to keep making a variety of friends."

"Any more about the tenth grader with the jacket?"

Molly frowned. "I made her give it back to him, and apparently, her short-lived popularity ended that moment. I'm to blame."

"You're a good mother. There's no reason for a boy that much older to pay attention to a young girl." He cast around for a way to cheer her up. "Have you seen what they've done with the farm?"

She shook her head, put her hands on her hips, and did an appreciative turn around. "It looks like a great place."

"It is. Want me to give you a tour?"

"Sure!" She reached out and touched his arm, and the feeling of it travelled right to his heart. "Thanks," she said, seeming totally unaffected.

He cleared it with Enid Bigby, matriarch of the farm, and they headed toward the barn.

"It's a lavender operation." He stepped aside so she could enter. Bundles of lavender hung from hooks on the rafters, and a large metal vat dominated one corner of the room. "They make lavender oils and such."

"I never thought about where lavender comes from." She inhaled one of the drying stalks. "That's an amazing idea. Can we see the fields?"

"Sure, though their biggest blooming season is past. You aren't exactly a farm girl, are you?"

"No." She wrinkled her nose ruefully. "I've spent my adult life in the city, and my childhood, too. Arcadia Valley is the smallest town I ever lived in."

"Are you happy with your move back?"

She nodded, but her eyes clouded. "In most ways, yes. But it's an adjustment for both of us."

He had to ask. "Did you leave behind someone special in Cleveland?"

She glanced at him and then shook her head. "Between working and mothering Trina, there hasn't been a lot of time for romance." She hesitated, then added, "I'm surprised you haven't settled down with someone. You're such a family man."

He laughed. "You mean I'm a stick in the mud."

"Did I say that?" She laughed up at him, and then her face got serious. "No, you know what I mean.

You believe in family. It's so important to you. I'd think you would want children of your own."

"I do. I just haven't met the right woman yet."

Or maybe, he was walking along next to her right now.

Was he?

"We never talked about what happened by the river," he heard himself say.

"Javier…"

"We should talk about it. Do you regret what happened?"

She looked out across the fields and then turned to him. "I don't regret it, but it scares me."

"Why?"

"Because of all the walls between us. I can't afford to get my heart broken again."

He blinked. "Did I break it before?"

"Of course! You told me you never wanted to see me again, called me terrible names…"

"You betrayed me! Cheated on me! I thought I was being generous to try to forgive you…"

"Don't make assumptions about what happened," she said, and opened her mouth as if to say more.

"Hey, everyone, we're going to pray and then eat," came a loud call from the gathering.

She turned toward the others, and he put a hand on her shoulder. "I'm sorry I got upset. Can we talk more sometime?"

She nodded, head bent, but didn't speak.

Javier's heart was in turmoil as they headed back to the group. After Pastor Harris prayed, everyone dug in. Javier sat with Daniel and his girls, and Molly and Trina with new church friends. Which was how it should be. There was no need for them to be together all the time. He didn't need to keep looking over at her to see what she was doing, whom she was talking to.

Back at the food tables for a piece of pie, he wasn't thrilled to find Molly's Aunt Lisa next to him, cutting herself a tiny slice. "Do you have a minute to talk?" she asked.

Something in her voice didn't sit right. "I... Daniel needs me with the twins." He didn't want to interact with Lisa. He didn't trust her.

"This won't take long." She tugged him aside. "Come on. Sit with me. I'm all alone."

"Where's Dale?" he asked uneasily.

"Oh, he's not well enough to come." She waved a hand as if her husband didn't matter. "Sit down."

He didn't. "What's this about, Lisa?"

"I just want to say," she said quietly, "that Molly tends to lie. I'd suggest taking her version of events with a grain of salt."

He cocked his head to one side. "Why are you telling me this?"

She looked down at the table, her forehead wrinkled. "I feel responsible for her character flaws, since I helped raise her."

Javier was starting to think Molly might not have as many character flaws as he'd believed. But something made him want to stay and listen to Lisa, even though he didn't trust her. He'd be better equipped to make decisions if he had all the information. "Yeah?"

"I noticed the two of you getting closer, and I figure she must be feeding you a line in order for that to happen."

"Lisa, this isn't...."

"Wait." She stood and leaned closer to him. "You're an honorable man, Javier, and I'd like to see you do well. I'm just saying, don't be gullible. Don't trust her."

Javier frowned. He didn't want to listen to vague, non-specific accusations.

At the same time, what Lisa was saying fit into the way he'd lived his life for years. *Women can't be trusted. Red flag. Caution advised.*

"The pie contest!" someone said. "Everyone gather 'round."

"There's a pie contest?" This was new.

"Oh, it's not a big deal," Lisa said, getting up. "Though I did win last year, with my apple pie."

They went along with the crowd, and Molly came to stand nearby. Obviously, she didn't know what Lisa had been saying, and she gave her aunt a friendly smile.

"What's going on?" she asked.

"Nothing real official," Pastor Harris said. "It's just, some of the men came up with the idea as a way to get more pie at the church dinner."

Molly laughed. "That was creative!"

"But The Grannies didn't think they were doing it right, so they took over."

"Who are The Grannies?"

Someone else turned back. "A bunch of gun-toting, 80-year-old martial arts experts."

"Including Enid Bigby, who owns this farm."

Lisa had stepped away to talk to someone, and Molly moved a little closer to Javier. He sidestepped in her direction, too. He liked having her near.

The grannies took the podium and held up three pies. "Here are the winning candidates."

The crowd cheered.

"Ruth Baxter... last year's winner, Lisa Abbott, and... Molly Abbott, Lisa's niece!"

"Oh, no," Molly said beside him.

Instantly he guessed what was wrong.

"Can I disqualify myself? Can you say you got sick from eating my pie?"

But it was too late. The pies were cut, and three pieces placed in front of each of the Grannies.

The women made a show of tasting and consulting, and soon they came up with a conclusion.

"We're judging this apple pie to be the best! Made by our new resident in Arcadia Valley, Molly Abbott!"

Molly stepped forward. "It's mine, but I give credit to my aunt. She taught me to make it."

"We love it when family traditions are passed down," one of the grannies, a woman named Mona, said happily.

Molly looked sick, and understandably so. Aunt Lisa was glaring their way with pure venom.

Javier wasn't going to listen to another word the woman said.

But he couldn't help wondering if there was a grain of truth to Lisa's accusations about Molly being dishonest.

# CHAPTER TEN

WHEN MOLLY ENTERED MARIA'S living room and saw Veronica, Kate Groves, and Charlotte MacGregor taking off their coats, tears welled up in her eyes. "Thank you guys for meeting at the last minute," she said, and there were hugs all around.

"Of course. We do this for each other."

"Come into the kitchen and meet my mom," Maria said, and Molly followed her friend into that amazing kitchen.

"This is my mom, and the girls tend to call her Mama Beatriz," Maria said, putting a hand on the arm of an older woman who stood at a cutting board.

Beatriz turned to face Molly, smiling. She wore a red-and-beige head wrap, which Molly at first thought was a fashion statement. But then she noticed that Beatriz didn't have eyebrows or eyelashes, and her face was pale, shiny and puffy. Uh-oh. Chemo.

Beatriz wiped her hand on a dishtowel and held it out to shake Molly's, her eyes warm. "So you're the spitfire who's been getting Mr. Javier Quintana to change his mind about food?"

"With your daughter's help, yes. It's nice to meet you." Molly gestured toward the cutting board. "Is that jicama?"

"Yes, we love it. I'm getting together a tray of vegetables for the group."

"I'm so in love with this kitchen," Molly confided as she put down her plate of cookies. "I feel bad about bringing something unhealthy."

Beatriz chuckled. "Believe me, we love us some cookies, too. Thanks for bringing them." She hesitated, then added, "when you have cancer, you enjoy every treat and happy moment you can find."

"I'm sorry." Molly squeezed the older woman's shoulder, gently. "That must be so hard."

"It's stage three, so the treatments are tough," Beatriz said. "But Maria's been a rock. She researched all kinds of things for me and that's why we started eating organic."

"I'm sure it's better for healing." Now Molly felt even worse about her unhealthy cookies.

"I'm sure, too, now that I've seen the research." Beatriz perched on a stool. "Studies have compared Latinos born here in the US, like us, with those who recently immigrated. Despite the poverty and lack of health care for a lot of new immigrants, their health is much better. Less cancer, less heart disease, healthier babies. Researchers call it the Latino advantage."

"And it's because of diet?" Molly leaned forward, intrigued.

"Maria and I are sure it is, although the scientists haven't caught up yet." Beatriz chuckled. "So we've gone back to ancestral foods. Lots of fruits and vegetables, corn tortillas, beans. I think it's helping."

"It makes a lot of sense to me."

Maria burst back into the kitchen. "Are you talking food? Mom has the zeal of the new convert."

"I might, too. I'd like to hear more about the research you've done, maybe even include some of the information—and the foods—on the menu at El Corazon."

"We'll see how well that goes over," Maria said, laughing.

Molly hugged her. "You're going to be such a resource going forward!"

"Thank you for saying that. But now..." She glanced from Molly to her mother. "Come on. We need to get started so we have time to pray."

Maria's handsome husband waved as he carried little Tomasito out of the room. "Have fun, ladies."

They dug into the simple food everyone had brought, the vegetables Beatriz had cut, and Molly's cookies. Once their snacking reduced to nibbling, Maria clapped her hands. "Attention, ladies! We're all busy, so let's get right down to business. I called you today because our sister in Christ and a new member of this group, Molly, is having a hard time of it and craves your prayer."

"What's going on?" Charlotte asked.

Molly sat back in her chair and looked around the circle of faces. She didn't know these women well yet, and for a moment, she wished she'd just gone it alone, like usual.

But if she wanted to build a life for herself and Trina in Arcadia Valley, she needed friends, a community of believers. She drew in a shaky breath and then held up a hand so she could tick her challenges off on her fingers. "First, the restaurant's debut with the new menu is happening next week."

"That's going to be so great!" said Charlotte.

"We'll all come support you," Kate added.

"It's going to be good, but I don't blame Molly for being stressed," Veronica said. "The restaurant has been the way it is for a long time, and there are people in the community, a few, who think everything should stay the way it was when..." She swallowed. "When Mom and Dad were alive."

Beatriz reached out and rubbed circles on Veronica's back. "You lost them too young. What do *you* think about the changes?"

Molly watched Veronica. If she wasn't really on board...

"Oh, I think it's great," Veronica said. "And Mom, at least, would have wanted to change with the times. It's just, if you know my brother Javier, you'll know he's a real traditionalist."

"*Plus* he and Molly have a history," Maria added. "I don't mean to gossip, but I think everyone in town knows about it, and if they don't, Molly's Aunt Lisa is happy to tell them."

Molly's stomach twisted. "I don't know why she's so mad at me. After my parents were killed, she didn't want to take me in, I know that. But it's like she hates me now."

"So we'll pray for Javier's mind to be opened, and Lisa's heart to be softened." Maria was taking notes. "What else is going on?"

"My daughter, Trina." She'd seemed better tonight, happy to go spend the evening with Laura and Raquel, but Molly still felt uneasy about her. "She's twelve, and she's had some struggles settling in to a new school. I'm just hoping she'll find a group of friends who are kind and have good values."

Maria's mother put a hand on Molly's arm. "When your child is suffering, it's worse than anything that happens to your own self. I know how hard that can be."

Tears welled up in Molly's eyes. Simple kindness and compassion. How long had it been since she'd felt it?

She looked around the circle of women and saw no judgment, nothing but support and budding friendship. It gave her courage to continue on. "There's something else, too. I... something happened in the past." She looked down at her hands, twisting the hem of her sweater. "I... something awful happened to me, and I'm afraid I brought it on myself. I didn't mean to, but I was a lonely young girl and I thought the attention was just kindness."

She stole a glance up at Veronica, then Maria. The women she knew best, and if there was condemnation...

But Veronica came and knelt by Molly's side, Maria stood behind her, hands on Molly's shoulders, and Beatriz took her hand.

"You don't have to answer this," Veronica said, "but are you talking about how Trina was conceived?"

Molly hunched in on herself, closing her eyes against the tears that burned her eyes. She'd never revealed the story outside of a counselor's office. Her heart pounded and her palms grew slippery-damp. "I was... forced, by someone I knew and trusted."

"Oh, Molly." Maria wrapped her arms around Molly from behind as Kate and Charlotte came to lay hands on her as well. "That's how Trina came to be?"

Molly blinked back the tears. "She's the blessing from it." Her voice sounded so hoarse, but she wanted them to know she had no ambivalence about her daughter. "She's the joy of my life."

Beatriz leaned closer. "You said you thought you might have brought it on yourself. But you were how old?"

"Seventeen." Shame washed over her. "Not a little girl. I didn't... I thought he was just being kind but... I liked the gifts and the attention."

Her stomach quaked and her shoulders felt rigid.

The other women were silent.

They were judging her. Of course they were. She'd done a horrible thing, encouraging Petey.

"Just... please, don't tell anyone," she whispered, looking at their faces for the first time.

Each of them had tears running down her face.

"Oh, Molly, I'm so sorry," Veronica said.

"That's what predators do," Maria sounded angry. "They groom their victims with gifts and attention. They choose girls who are vulnerable."

"It's true," Beatriz said. "Their intent is to make the victim blame herself. But, poor child, it is not your fault."

"This was an adult man?" Charlotte asked.

Molly nodded. "Old enough to be my father," she choked out.

"The shame is all on him," Maria said firmly. "Even if you'd consented, it would have been a crime because you were underage. But you said he forced you."

"I fought as hard as I could," she whispered, "but

I couldn't stop him. He was big and strong." And then the dam broke and she was sobbing. "I couldn't stop him."

The women clustered around her, whispering words of comfort or crying themselves.

*Wait a second.* They hadn't pulled away. They'd come closer.

"Lord Jesus, bring your blessing on Molly," came Beatriz's firm voice. "Help her to shed her shame and to know the truth of what happened to her."

"Help her feel your love in her heart."

"Let her know she's forgiven for any mistakes she made."

The prayers went on and the women stayed close, their hands on Molly, and a miraculous lightening came to her. A burden she'd been carrying since that horrible afternoon when Trina was conceived.

Yes, she'd made mistakes, but they were forgiven. She was loved. By these Christian women and by God.

Finally, as the words and the tears slowed down, Maria brought them back to the rest of their prayers. "Please, Lord, strengthen Trina against all the challenges she faces in school and with friends."

"Bring success to El Corazon, so it can become again a gathering place for the community, a place of heart."

Slowly, the women went back to their seats. They all held hands and a couple of the others asked for prayer for concerns they had. They prayed healing on Beatriz and success in a library board meeting for Charlotte. And Molly was able to let her own concerns go and pray wholeheartedly for the other women.

When they all opened their eyes and looked at each other, Maria laughed a little. "If my makeup looks as bad as the rest of you, I've got to clean up before my husband sees me. Be right back with tissues and makeup remover."

Winding down from the intensity of prayer, Molly felt a twinge of worry and shyness. She'd bared her heart to these women she didn't know well. They'd been kind, but would they look at her differently now?

But as Maria returned with tissues, Veronica touched Molly's arm. "Javier doesn't know about any of this, does he?"

"No. I... Aunt Lisa made me leave town right away." She swallowed. "She blamed me for what happened."

Veronica's eyes narrowed. "I'm trying not to hate that woman, but I'm having a hard time."

"If it really wasn't my fault... and if Javier knew... "

"He'd go after the guy." Veronica looked grim. "I would, myself. He's not... is he still in the area?"

"He's dead."

"Then God can judge." Veronica frowned. "Does

Trina know?"

"That's the problem. Lisa has hinted at the truth to her."

"With her own twist on it, I'm sure."

"Right, so..." Molly chewed on her lip. "Can I really trust everyone to keep this confidential?"

"Absolutely. What's said in the prayer group, stays in the prayer group. So don't worry about that."

Maria put a hand on Molly's arm. "You have some hard conversations coming. I'll continue to pray for you and Trina."

"And I for you. Thank you so much for bringing me into the group." There were hugs all around, and promises of support. Molly felt wrung out like a washrag, but cleansed.

They hadn't condemned her. They didn't think it was her fault.

Maybe it wasn't her fault.

Whatever the culpability, God loved her in spite of her mistakes.

She needed to have those difficult conversations. With Trina, and maybe, with Javier.

MOLLY DROVE HOME lighthearted, but the sight of Aunt Lisa's car in front of her cottage sent a foreboding chill down her spine. She parked and trotted up the steps.

"She's fine," Lisa's voice came from one of the porch rocking chairs. "Sit down."

"She's supposed to be at Mariana's. What are you doing here?"

"I told her you wanted me to pick her up, and she believed me."

Molly rushed inside and opened Trina's bedroom door.

Trina was curled up on her bed, sleeping.

Molly checked to make sure she was truly asleep and okay, kissed her and prayed over her, and then went back outside. "What's this all about, Aunt Lisa? What are you doing here?"

"I was expecting you to take your... your *love child* and go back where you came from, but here you still are."

"I don't understand. What do you have against me and Trina?"

Aunt Lisa threw up her hands. "If you don't know by now!"

Molly shook her head and sank down into the rocking chair beside her aunt. "I don't know. I truly don't understand."

"First, you took my husband away from me. And then—"

"Wait. Whoa. I didn't take Uncle Dale away from you."

Lisa crossed her arms and glared at Molly. "When

you came to live with us, he started coming home from work on time again. Having dinner at home. Working around the house on the weekends."

"He didn't do those things before I came?"

"No, he didn't do those things before you came! He worked late, and ran around with the boys, and golfed all weekend. I never saw him."

Molly figured there was quite a bit more to the story, but still, she was gaining insight. "You were jealous? Of me?"

"No, of course not! It was just ridiculous, and it made me look ridiculous. Asking about *your* day, buying *you* a new dress..."

"But..." Molly trailed off. What was the use of pointing out that Aunt Lisa had started nagging and complaining the moment Uncle Dale came through the door? That she bought herself so many designer clothes that Uncle Dale always looked sad and alarmed when the bills came due?

Aunt Lisa saw what she wanted to see. Never before had that been so clear to Molly.

"Now you're back in town, and wanting to move in with him. In *my* place!"

"No, not in your place. I was just trying to help out. While you were gone." She waved an arm toward the cottage. "We're settled here. We're not going to impose on you and Uncle Dale."

"Everyone in town talks about how wonderful you

are, how selfless. How you take him to his doctor appointments and make him sugar-free pies and—"

"I'm sorry that's been bothering you so much." Molly opened her mouth to say she wouldn't do it anymore, and then closed it again. She didn't want to promise that, not when Uncle Dale needed her.

"I want you out of here," Lisa continued. "If you won't leave on your own, I'll tell everyone who Trina's father is, and how you seduced a married man just so you could get pregnant and get out of town!"

Molly felt the words as blows, but alongside the hurt, red-hot anger flowed. "You think I *wanted* to get pregnant? That I *wanted* Petey to do what he did? You saw me! You saw I was bruised and bleeding and crying, practically destroyed. And rather than comforting me, you slapped me and sent me away! Who does that to an innocent young girl?" As she spoke, Molly's anger grew bigger and wider until it seemed to fill her whole vision. "You're the one who did wrong. Not as much as Petey, but you hurt me terribly and left me without a soul in the world. If it weren't for Uncle Dale paying for that home for unwed mothers, I'd have been on the street."

"It would have served you right. Don't you dare bring up Petey's name. It was your fault, all your fault, walking around with that cute little figure, showing off your youth and beauty when I was getting older by the day. I worked out, I had my face done, and still he preferred you!"

"Wait." Molly leaned forward and stared at her aunt. "*Who* preferred me? Uncle Dale... or Petey?"

Aunt Lisa pressed her lips tight together.

"Did you... " No. It couldn't be. Molly must have misunderstood. "Look. I don't understand why you felt jealous of a child. Uncle Dale loves you and always will. You're his wife. He's never stopped talking about how beautiful you are."

"Oh, don't try to placate me. I want you and Trina out of town. By tomorrow. Or I tell the whole town what you did." She exploded out of the rocker and ran to her car.

Molly stared after her, and then sat for a long time, rocking and looking up at the night sky. *What do I do now, Lord?*

JAVIER ENTERED EL CORAZON the next morning hoping to have the chance to think a little before anyone else arrived.

No such luck. There was Molly, working prep with Maria. Mounds of chopped onion and pepper were already beside them, and as he came in, Maria glanced up, saw him, and moved over to start making tortillas for the day.

Molly was pale, and it looked like she'd been crying, but her expression was steady and resolute. "Soft reopening day," she reminded him, as if he didn't know.

"Where's Trina?" he asked.

Molly nodded sideways toward the dining room. "She has a big history project she's working on."

Which meant this was his best chance to speak to Molly alone. His heart pounding with a mixture of hurt, anger, and concern, he came over and stood across the prep table from her, grabbing a couple of blocks of cheese to shred. "I need to talk to you about what happened right before you left town," he said.

Her eyebrows rose almost to her hairline. "What do you know about it?"

"I know that I had the whole thing wrong, and that you deliberately kept the truth from me."

"Who told you?" she asked, rather than denying it.

He blew out a breath, debating the ethics of the situation. Lisa had asked for his silence, but he hadn't promised it. "It's not important, is it?" he asked, keeping his voice mild, calm.

Molly didn't answer. Instead, she peeled off her plastic gloves and stalked over to Maria. "I thought the prayer group was confidential."

"It is," Maria said, glancing over at Javier.

"He knows something." Molly didn't bother to keep her voice low.

"I could swear it wasn't one of our ladies." Maria looked over at Javier. "Who told you, and what did they tell you?"

But they were interrupted by Pablo's arrival. The older cook came in and looked around, his forehead wrinkling, and Javier knew him well enough to immediately know why: there were all these people in his kitchen, doing things he hadn't approved, and to boot, the restaurant was trying out the new style today for the first time.

Javier cleared his throat. "Now that Pablo's here, I think those of us who aren't cooks should get out of here," he suggested.

"Good idea," Maria said promptly. But she softened her words with a pat on Molly's back. When had the two of them gotten so cozy?

"I'd like to talk to you," he said to Molly. "Come into the back dining room for a minute?"

She blew out a breath. "Let me check on Trina. I'll meet you there."

Veronica was in the back dining room, checking on the table setups. She lifted an eyebrow at Javier. "You ready for all the changes today?"

"I'm more ready for that than for this conversation," he murmured just as Molly came in.

Veronica looked from him to Molly. "Think I'll get out of here."

"It wasn't you who told him about... what I talked about last night," Molly asked Veronica. "Was it?"

"Of course not! I would never do that." Veronica

put an arm around Molly. "Remember, we're here for you."

Did everyone know about Molly's history but him? His sense of hurt and injustice was growing by the minute.

"First customers here in half an hour." Veronica slipped out of the room.

"It's not an ideal time to talk," Molly said.

"No. The ideal time would have been about thirteen years ago." He pulled out a chair. "Sit down."

She gave him an exasperated look, but did as he said. "Who told you," she asked again, "and what did they tell you? Was it Aunt Lisa?"

He nodded. "I know the source is biased. But if even part of what she told me is true..."

"Part of it is true," she said. "At least, I'm guessing so." She paused and drew a deep, shaky breath. "Did she tell you that Petey Jones was Trina's father?"

A huge sigh wooshed out of him. "Yes. Was he?" He'd hoped so hard that it wasn't so.

She nodded, looking at him levelly.

She didn't look ashamed. Her jaw was set, square, like she was clenching her teeth.

He looked away for a minute, trying to school the red tide of rage inside him. The thought of Petey Jones being with Molly... "He was twenty years older than you! What on earth would make you..."

She leaned forward. "Seduce him? Because I'm

sure that's what Aunt Lisa told you."

"She did, but... " He shook his head. "I just can't fathom that you would do that."

"I didn't." She drew in a deep breath. "I'm going to try to tell you what happened. I need for you to listen without saying anything, until I'm done."

He nodded.

"You probably remember how Petey liked to come over to Aunt Lisa's and Uncle Dale's. He was Uncle Dale's best friend, right? He was there all the time."

"I remember—" He wasn't supposed to talk. But a memory of the jovial man, pounding Dale's back and giving Lisa a big loud kiss, came back to him.

"Do you remember how he always had a gift for me, too? Stuffed animals, chocolates, a book?"

Again, he nodded.

"Not many people treated me that well," she said.

"I treated you well!"

She put a hand on his. "Oh, Javier, you did. You treated me perfectly, and I loved you so much."

Her words washed over him, a tide of gladness and pain. "Then why—" He broke off. "Sorry. I'll let you explain."

"You were my boyfriend," she said. "Mr. Petey was like a father. I missed my own dad so much, you know that. Yes, Uncle Dale was wonderful. He filled that role as best he could, but... Aunt Lisa kept a pretty tight rein on him. The one time he bought me a fancy new calculator I needed for math, she made him take it back. She'd get furious if he ever gave me a hug or a high five."

Javier wanted to scream at her to cut to the chase, to get on with the story. But that wasn't how women operated. Veronica had pounded that into him, and he'd learned to listen to her, and his mother, and his grandmother for a different type of truth.

"One afternoon, when I was home alone, Petey brought me chocolates, and he really wanted me to eat them right away." She drew in a shaky sigh. "They were good. The fancy kind. I ate three of them."

Javier's heart felt like a stone.

"When I woke up, we were in my room and he was... well." She looked away. Her knuckles were white on the edge of the table. "He assaulted me. I... " She looked at him and her eyes were black holes. "I tried to fight, Javier, I did. But my arms and legs were heavy, weighed down. Mostly, I was confused. I couldn't understand why Mr. Petey was in the room when I wasn't dressed and why he was saying such mean things to me, when he'd always been so nice."

"If I had a gun, I'd shoot that man." He slammed his fist into his hand.

She jerked back as if afraid.

He drew in a couple of calming breaths, pried her hand off the edge of the table and took it in both of his. Leaned toward her, but it somehow didn't seem right to try to hold her. "I'm sorry. So sorry that happened to you." Underneath his aching compassion, a sharp edge of anger remained at the man who'd done this to her, but he knew now wasn't the time to express it. "What happened next?"

She stared down at the tabletop. "I don't know if you remember how I got really sick right before... before I left town? Missed a couple of weeks of school?"

He did remember.

She nodded. "That's why."

"Did you go to the police?"

She shook her head.

"To Lisa and Dale?"

She swallowed convulsively. "I went to Aunt Lisa. She... she blamed me. Hit me. Said I'd led him on and enticed him into it."

"Like she told me." Javier wiped sweat from his forehead. He thought back to the girl Molly had been. She hadn't had it in her to do as Lisa had said, to seduce a married man. If anything, she'd been more naive than most girls her age. Javier had been her first boyfriend, and he'd seen her innocence for himself.

It had made him protective. Obviously, it had had a different effect on Petey.

One question burned in him. "Why didn't you tell me? Didn't you trust that I'd take care of you, help you?"

She looked at him, biting her lip.

"We were so close. You could have told me. Should have told me."

"I was afraid."

"Of me?"

"Aunt Lisa said no one would believe me. And Javier, she was probably right. I mean, she didn't believe me. He was a popular man in the community. Even Uncle Dale... well, I couldn't bring myself to tell him, because Mr. Petey was his best friend."

"But if no one told, he was free to do that to other girls."

She closed her eyes. "I've felt guilty about that for years. Fortunately, he succumbed to his own drug issues not long after that."

It was all coming together for him now. "I'd heard a rumor his death was drug related."

"Me, too." She clutched his hand like a lifeline. "Don't you see, Javier, I wanted to tell you, but I couldn't." She swallowed. "I'm *not* a Quintana with a whole supportive family behind me. I was an orphan with an aunt who called me a lying tramp, and I believed her. I believed it was my fault. In fact..." She paused. "I'm only learning now, with God's help, that it wasn't."

"Wow."

She lifted her hands, palms up. "You're shocked."

He nodded. "This has changed my whole world."

"And your whole view of me?"

He squeezed her hand. "I have a lot to think about. But the biggest thing is...I'm sad you were hurt that way. And..." It was only now sinking in. "I thought you'd cheated on me. I jumped to conclusions, and I'm ashamed of myself."

"What were you supposed to think? How could you have known?"

He let his head sink down, propping it on his knuckles. "When I came to see you, and realized you were expecting, I lost my head."

She nodded.

"So you had the baby alone. Trina." The implications were crashing in on him. "How much does she know?"

"She knows her dad was a bad man, but that doesn't mean she's bad."

"That's all?"

She nodded. "So far, but... being back here, and with Aunt Lisa on the warpath, that's probably going to change."

"Mariana? Laura and Raquel? Because they're..."

"Trina's half-sisters. But nobody knows. Yet."

"Wow. Complicated."

The doors to the dining room burst open and two teenaged girls, probably high school seniors, approached the table, dressed in black pants and white shirts. "Your sister said we should report to you," one of them said to Javier.

"We're training as wait staff tonight. She said you knew where the aprons and name tags are?"

Javier blinked. Girls? As waiters?

But things changed. And things weren't always what you thought they were. He stood. "Sure. Come on back."

"I've got to get out there too, and help." Molly stood.

He looked into her steady, dark eyes and realized what strength was there. What power.

She'd just told him about the worst thing that could happen to a woman, short of death. Now she was drawing herself up to do her job.

So they went, and they did it, and it was good. The food went over well and the new wait staff was going to be great.

The idea of the restaurant's traditions changing suddenly didn't seem as crucial or disastrous. Not compared to what had happened to Molly.

Was it true that she couldn't have told him, that he wouldn't have believed her?

He thought of himself, how he'd been then. How rigid and proud. He was still that way. But the hurt to Molly... all the years they'd missed... it haunted him as he went through the motions of welcoming customers and supervising staff and solving problems.

After the last customer had left, he sat in the dining

room trying to focus, to go through the receipts while the rest of the staff cleaned up. Suddenly, there was an outcry in the kitchen.

Molly burst out into the dining room. "Have you seen Trina?"

"No." He stood, alarmed at her expression. "What's wrong?"

Molly's shoulders sank down. "I'm afraid something happened. She's gone. She's missing."

# CHAPTER ELEVEN

MOLLY GRABBED A TABLE, suddenly unsteady on her feet. Where could Trina be? Where to look? Waves of terror washed over her numb core.

"Pablo. Kitchen. Look everywhere." Javier yelled orders. "Maria. Back of the restaurant. Restrooms. Veronica. Get Alex and Daniel on the phone and get them over here." His hand clamped on Molly's arm. "Come on. Let's search the parking lot and your car and then we'll go from there."

She let him lead her, shaking her head to clear the fog, her heart sliced through with pain and panic. In the parking lot, the warm air enveloped her while gravel scraped underfoot. She had the inane thought that at least Trina wouldn't be cold. "Trina! Trina, honey, come here." Her voice sounded choked, too quiet.

"Trina!" Javier yelled it, much louder. "Trina! If you can hear me, come to your mom's car!"

No sound except the cicadas.

"Get out your keys." Javier thrust her purse at

her—when had he picked that up? She dug to the bottom, grabbed her keys, then handed them to him. He clicked open her car and they both searched. Empty.

"Who would she be with?" He found her phone and gave it to her. "Call Dale and Lisa."

"What? Okay. Yes." She clicked the contact and the phone buzzed.

Javier was talking on his own phone, low and rapid Spanish.

Uncle Dale picked up. "Hey, Molly girl, how'd it go?" he asked in his jovial voice. "Did you get a lot of customers?"

Tears stung Molly's eyes and tightened her throat. "Trina's missing," she choked out. "Is she with you?"

"No. No, she hasn't been here." Concern threaded through his words. "Are you sure? Could she have taken off with a friend and forgot to tell you?"

Images of Trina's new friends, Raquel and Laura and Maisie, flashed through Molly's mind. "I'm pretty sure. Is Aunt Lisa there?"

"No, she went out awhile back."

Foreboding clutched Molly's chest. "Could you call her? But don't come looking." She didn't want Uncle Dale to endanger himself. "Stay there so if Trina comes to your house, there's someone home."

"I will. And I'll get ahold of Lisa, one way or the other. Anything else I can do?"

"Do you know Maisie Felton?"

"Know her mom. Want me to call them?"

"Yes, please. Just ask if Maisie has any idea where Trina might be, and let me know if you find anything out."

As soon as he agreed, she clicked off and the terror coursed through her again. If Trina had taken off down the highway, hitchhiked like kids had done in a TV show they'd watched recently...

Javier took her hand and tugged her back toward the restaurant. "No luck?"

"Uncle Dale doesn't know anything, and Aunt Lisa's out." She looked up at him.

His mouth tightened. "We'll find her."

"I'm wondering about Trina's friends."

"I reached Raquel and she sounded... funny. I think we should go over there."

"Yes. Okay." Maybe Trina was hiding out there, and the girls didn't want to tell on her.

They went inside El Corazon to find Maria, Pablo, and Veronica clustered together.

"Anyone find anything?"

"No," Pablo said, "but I will contact the new waitresses. They were talking to her, and they're young. Maybe they noticed something."

"I'll get the prayer group on it," Maria said. "And my mom. We'll drive the streets of Arcadia Valley and stop anywhere teenagers gather."

"Alex and Patricia are on their way," Veronica said. "When they get here, we'll drive to the cottages and start hunting that whole area. We'll check the road along the way. Daniel can't leave his girls, but he's contacting the police, state and local. He'll also call Pastor Harris, see what the church can do."

A tiny flame of hope warmed Molly's chest. People were helping. With all these people helping, they'd find Trina. Wouldn't they?

She looked up at Javier, grateful beyond words for his support and leadership. "We should go to Raquel and Laura."

"I'll drive. Everyone, stay in touch. Call me or Molly if you see or hear anything."

Their drive to Mariana's house was silent. Molly kept her eyes fixed on the side of the road. It was a long walk to the Valley Cottages, but if Trina had been upset, she might have tried it.

"Why would she have run away?" she asked aloud. "Do you think..."

Javier turned into the cottages. "Did she overhear us talking?"

Molly reviewed their conversation in her mind and her heart rate accelerated. "Oh, no."

"It would be a tough way for her to find out." Javier braked hard in front of Mariana's cottage, and they both got out and half ran to the front door.

Mariana answered, her eyes red. When she saw

Molly, her mouth tightened.

"We're looking for Trina," Javier said. "She's gone missing. Can we come in and talk to the girls?"

"You can." Mariana held the door for Javier to walk inside, but stepped in front of Molly. "I don't want you in this house."

Lisa had gotten to her. "If one of your girls were missing," Molly said, "I'd do anything to help."

"To think you moved here with that child—" Mariana put her hands over her face. "Petey's child. The half-sister of my girls." She uncovered her face and stared at Molly. "How could you? How could you do it?"

The old familiar shame roiled inside Molly, but she focused on the feelings she'd had when the prayer group had surrounded her. Peace. Love. Healing.

She'd been a victim. Mariana was a victim, too. God loved both of them. "Look, we'll talk about what happened all those years ago, but right now, I *have* to find Trina. Let me talk to your girls."

"No." Mariana crossed her arms. "I won't let evil in my home."

"You already did, when you married Petey," Molly heard her own voice, shaking, pitched too high. "Did you turn Trina out, too? Did she come here and you said something awful to her?" Molly's heart pounded and her fists clenched. "If you hurt my little girl—"

"I wouldn't. It's *you* I'm angry with."

"Consider the source of your information." She tried to push past Mariana.

The other woman gripped her arm, sharp nails digging in. "I said, you're not welcome in my house."

"And I said, let me by." Inside, she could see Javier in the doorway of one of the bedrooms. He turned and beckoned to Molly.

She shook off the other woman's hands. "I'm sorry," she said as she elbowed her way into the room.

"I'm calling the police! You stay away from my daughters!"

"I won't touch them." Molly rushed to where Javier was standing and looked past him to Laura and Raquel, both sitting on a bed. "Do you know where Trina is?"

"No!" Laura drew her knees up to her chin, wrapping her arms around her legs.

"But," Raquel said, and turned to her sister. "Tell her what you do know. Come on. What if something happens to her? How will you feel?"

Molly slid past Javier and into the bedroom, dropping to her knees beside the bed. "Please, Laura. Tell me what you know. Please." Dimly, behind her, she heard Javier's voice, remonstrating with Mariana.

"Is my dad her dad, too?" Laura asked.

Molly closed her eyes for a moment and then opened them. If only she'd handled things differently.

"Yes. And we need to talk about how it happened. But not until Trina is safe."

"You acted like our friend!" Laura snarled. "When really, you tried to steal our father from our mother."

She couldn't refute that lie, not now. There wasn't time. "What do you know about Trina?"

Raquel sat upright, cross-legged on the twin bed. "I'm mad at you, too, but you need to know what Laura heard. She called Trina after your aunt came over here and told us. Trina said she just heard, too, and she'd called Terrance McKinley."

Molly gasped. "The tenth grader? The one with the jacket?"

"And a car," Raquel said. "He's not a nice boy. He was going to pick her up, but I don't know where they were going."

"It serves her right," Laura said, but Molly was already turning to Javier. "How can we find them?" *Trina, Trina,* her heart screamed. *Please, don't let it happen to you, too.*

JAVIER DROVE DOWN the canyon road at a barely-safe speed. He hadn't been able to help Molly in her distress all those years ago, hadn't known about it and had judged her wrongly afterward.

He wasn't going to make the same mistake with her daughter. He had to help her, find her.

"Hurry. Hurry." Molly was beside him, leaning

forward, hand on the dashboard.

His phone buzzed, then buzzed again.

She picked it up and looked at the screen. "Alex and Patricia are on their way. Veronica's talking to Terrance's mom but..." Another message buzzed in and she clicked it. "Terrance isn't home, and she doesn't know where he is."

If only his hunch proved right, and the pair was at the most isolated makeout point in the county.

He wondered if Molly remembered that they'd come down here a couple of times, too.

Of course, they'd been in love, and they'd only been out to get a little unsupervised time together, to hold each other and talk, share their dreams.

Terrance, he feared, was after something else entirely.

They squealed into the parking lot and jolted to a stop beside two other vehicles. "Wait for me," he called when Molly jumped out of the car. "There could be all kinds of low-lifes down here."

"That's what I'm afraid of!" Her voice rose to shrillness. "Come on!"

Javier shone his bright flashlight into each of the adjoining cars, but both were empty. "Find out what Terrance drives."

Molly bit her lip and clicked the text into her phone while Javier searched the parking lot, behind rocks and scrub pines. Molly joined him, peering under branches and leaning over the ledge. But there was no sign of the kids, no sound.

Molly's phone buzzed. "Veronica says Terrance drives a brown Chevy," she said. "That's the car, right?" She pointed back at the car nearest theirs.

"That's it. They must have headed down toward the caves." But which path to take?

"Help us, Lord," he prayed, and chose the one in the middle. "Come on. We'll find them."

Molly's breath came in ragged gasps. She stared at him with wide eyes.

"We'll find them," he repeated.

He only hoped it was in time.

MOLLY STUMBLED DOWN the path ahead of Javier, barely aware of the rocks and shadows. When they reached the river, the full moon traced a path across it.

The beauty reminded Molly to pray even as she quickened her pace. "Help Trina, Lord," she said out loud. "Please, help her. Keep her safe."

They emerged out onto one of river's beaches, about fifty feet wide and rocky, with steep rock walls above.

In the walls were caves, some easily accessible and some higher up, requiring a climb. Generations of young people had used them for privacy or partying. A few had been hurt falling down the rocks after too much drinking.

Again, Molly prayed for Trina's safety.

Javier climbed to one of the lower, larger rock caves and shone his light around. "Nobody."

"Trina! Trina!" Molly called, and the sound echoed back across the water. "Come on. It's Mom. You're not in trouble."

Javier ducked under an overhanging rock and swung his way up to another secluded indentation. There was a sound.

"Trina!" Molly stepped on a rock behind Javier. "Help me up!"

"It's not them," he said back to her, and then addressed someone in the cave. "Did you guys see another couple here?"

Molly's stomach turned at the thought of Trina— her innocent, childish, naive little girl—as part of a couple.

"No, man," came an irritated male voice. "Leave us alone."

Javier signaled for her to climb back down and he followed, as nimble as a mountain goat. His phone buzzed and he looked at it and texted a quick response. "Patricia and Alex are here," he told Molly. "They're taking the right-hand path. It goes off way off east."

Way off. She didn't want her daughter to be way off. And what if that brown car hadn't been Terrance's? What if Trina wasn't even here? What if

Terrance had taken her to some motel, or a friend's house?

Javier seemed to read her thoughts. "I think this is where he'd come. He's a kid, he doesn't have any money for gas or a room."

Molly nodded. "Trina! Trina! Hold on, we're coming to find you!"

But there was no answer, only another echo of her own voice.

"Come on, there's a pathway here to a cave that's further back," Javier said. "Although the only reason they'd go off that far..." He trailed off.

Was if Terrance wanted to be really isolated, and didn't want anyone to hear Trina. She swallowed hard. "Let's go."

They were climbing through what seemed to be a pile of rubble—falling, scraping knees and shins, breathing hard—when Molly heard it. A small, whimpering sound.

She put a hand on Javier's sleeve to still him. "Trina! Trina, it's Mom. Where are you?"

A weak shout came from above and in front of them, and Molly started scrambling straight up the rocks toward a black basalt cave opening.

Javier put a hand on her leg. "Wait. There might be an easier way."

"Trina!" Molly ignored him and called again, trying to gauge where the sounds were coming from. If it were only an animal...

"Mommy?" came a small, scared cry.

Molly climbed the ledge to where she heard the voice, her muscles working, finding fingerholds, barely noticing Javier boosting her from behind. Her arms and hands scraped rocks and sand. "Trina. Trina, hold on, I'm coming?"

"Mommy? It hurts."

Her heart breaking, Molly boosted herself the last few feet and into the mouth of the cave. There, huddled on her side with her arms around herself, was Trina.

"Oh, baby!" Molly ran and wrapped her arms around her child, tears flowing freely. "Oh, baby, you're alive!"

"It hurts," Trina whimpered.

"What hurts, sweetie? Where do you hurt?" She was dimly aware of Javier behind her, shining a flashlight and then turning it to the side, out of Trina's eyes.

"Where'd Terrance go?" he asked sharply. Too sharply, and Molly frowned back at him, telling him with her eyes not to upset Trina any more.

"I don't know, he ran off," Trina said. She sniffled a couple of times and sat up.

"What hurts?" Molly's heart was aching as she ran her hands over Trina's arms, trying to see in the light from Javier's flashlight.

"My wrist." Trina thrust her hand in front of Molly's face. "And my leg's bleeding from the rocks. And he tore my new shirt!"

Molly blew out a breath. No serious injuries, and thank the Lord Trina was able to be upset about a shirt. "Let's see your wrist."

"No, Mom, look at this! He grabbed my shirt and looked at my bra!" Trina's voice held full-on indignation now as she pointed at the neckline of her shirt, where a small piece of lace was torn. "So I kicked him like they taught us in that self-defense class back in Cleveland, remember?"

Molly swallowed down a semi-hysterical laugh. "I remember, honey." She'd been unsure of whether Trina, at ten, was too young for such a class, even a mother-daughter one, but she'd gone with her gut and signed them up.

*Thank you, Father.*

"But he had me by the wrist, so when he fell down, he twisted it. I pulled his hand off me by the pinkie, like they taught us. And it worked!"

Now Molly did laugh, just a little, through the tears running down her face.

Javier came forward and knelt beside Molly. "You did great," he said to Trina, putting an arm around Molly's shoulders for just a second.

"Then I was mad, so I kicked him again. He was almost crying!" Trina's eyes narrowed. "I told him, 'you can't do that to girls,' and he ran away."

"Oh, sweetheart, I am so proud of you." Molly's heart was full to bursting. If only she'd known to do what Trina had done. If only she'd had that confidence and self-awareness.

But then she wouldn't have this wonderful, spunky daughter. She looked upward and closed her eyes, overwhelmed.

"But afterwards, I got scared," Trina admitted. "I didn't like being here by myself and I didn't know how to get home. And it got so dark."

Molly hugged Trina again and kept an arm around her. "It's taken care of. We're going to get you out of here."

Javier took his button-down shirt off, leaving him wearing only a sleeveless undershirt. Using his teeth, he tore a long strip from the front of it. "Wrap this around her wrist," he told Molly. "I'm going to let people know she's been found. Then I can carry her down if she needs."

Yes, he certainly could, if the muscles on display were any indication.

"I can walk," Trina said. "My wrist hurts more than my leg."

"Hold it out." Molly wrapped the slightly swollen wrist and tucked the edges in. "There. Does that help?"

"Yeah. Mom, I can't believe he did that to me!"

"Think about what mistakes you made," Molly

said, forcing herself to be firm. "You should never have gone off with him."

"But I was mad!" Trina's expression clouded. "I heard what you said, back at the restaurant. Is that true, that Laura and Raquel's dad is my dad, too?"

Molly blew out a breath and looked over at Javier, but his face held the same uncertainty she felt. She hadn't meant to have this conversation in a cave on the edge of a river, but then again, was there a better place?

She took hold of her daughter's good hand and brushed back her hair. "It's true, honey. Did you hear about how it happened?"

Trina nodded, and her mouth twisted a little, like she was going to cry. Then she lifted her chin and shook her head a little. Clearly, she didn't want to delve too deeply into the emotions of her own conception. Which made sense. There was a time and place for that, probably a counselor's office.

"We'll talk more about this when you're ready," Molly promised.

"I was thinking about it when Terrance was trying to mess with me. I thought how you said you tried to fight, and I thought, I should fight, too. So I did."

"I'm so proud of you for that." She held Trina loosely in her arms now, trying to restrain the sobs that wanted to come out, to stay calm for the daughter she loved. "I want you to know that, as bad as my experience was, you're the blessing that came from it.

So I wouldn't change anything."

"Wow." Trina shook her head hard, like she couldn't take that much in. "So wait. Do I have sisters after all?"

Molly nodded. "In a very complicated way, yes, you do. But—"

"I know, they're mad at me. Or Laura is at least." Trina twisted around to look at Molly's face and frowned. "They think it was your fault and you were bad."

"I know." Molly brushed back Trina's hair. "It's confusing for everyone. So you and I, at least, are going to talk to a counselor to try to understand it all better. Maybe one day, Raquel and Laura will be able to come, too."

"Then we can be a family? Because I really want to have sisters."

Molly blew out a sigh. They weren't going to have a conventional family, but now wasn't the time to navigate the details. "We have to leave some of this in God's hands." She squeezed Trina's shoulders. "Right now, we need to get you home. Come on, Mr. Quintana will help us climb down."

"You can call him Javier, Mom," Trina said, rolling her eyes.

As waves of relief and happiness washed over Molly, she gave thanks for her feisty daughter's safety and spirit.

# CHAPTER TWELVE

JAVIER PULLED INTO the Valley Cottages, Molly beside him and Trina snoring lightly in the backseat, wrapped in a blanket. They'd already updated the police about Terrance. Now, he planned to help Molly get Trina inside and into bed and then spend some time talking to Molly. Or maybe just holding her.

He was still processing the fact that she hadn't cheated on him. And that she had been afraid to tell him the truth, afraid of his judgment.

He'd been rigid, a black and white thinker. Still was, in many ways. That had to change.

He turned the car toward Molly's cottage and jolted to a halt. A car was diagonally across the road, partially in the grass but still blocking the narrow throughway.

Molly jerked upright. "That's Aunt Lisa's car, isn't it?"

"Stay back." He put the car into park, got out, and approached the other car cautiously. Was Lisa still trying to get some kind of retribution?

A large figure was slumped into the steering wheel. Larger than Lisa. Javier's muscles tensed and he opened the driver's side door.

In the interior light he could see Dale, semi-conscious, his face grey. The man was gasping for breath.

Beside him, sprawled in the lowered passenger seat, was Lisa. She looked to be out, cold.

He beckoned to Molly and then turned back to Dale. "What's going on? Did you have a wreck?" He was no doctor, but basic first aid training from his army years told him this situation was well beyond his abilities.

"What's wrong?" Molly leaned over him. "Uncle Dale!"

"Call an ambulance," Javier said over his shoulder and leaned farther into the car, trying to see if he could make Dale more comfortable.

"Brought... her here... to apologize." Dale paused longer, taking a labored breath, his face twisting. "She... has... a problem."

Beside him, Lisa slept on. At least, he hoped she was just sleeping. "Make sure she's breathing," he said to Molly, and she moved instantly to the passenger side of the car and opened the door.

"She has a pulse, but it seems faint. What happened to her, Uncle Dale?"

"Drugs... first painkillers... then more." He struggled for breath and clutched at his chest.

Heart attack? "You can explain later." Javier's first aid training was coming back to him. "Do you have any aspirin?" he asked Molly.

"Back at the house. I'll get it." She took off running. "Make sure Trina's okay," she called over her shoulder.

Javier refastened Dale's seatbelt to keep him secure and then jogged back to his car. Trina was still sound asleep in the back seat. He hurried back with his phone and typed "heart attack symptoms" into the search engine. "Do you have pain in your arms or neck? Heavy chest?"

Dale nodded. "It's my heart," he said, and then his eyes fluttered closed.

"Did you take anything yet?"

A faint shake of the head seemed to be all Dale could manage.

He heard running footsteps and then Molly appeared with a bottle of aspirin. "How many?"

"One." He took the tablet and got in Dale's face. "Wake up. Chew this."

Dale's head rolled back and forth on his fleshy neck and his eyes fluttered open.

"Chew this. It's important. It'll limit the damage."

The older man opened his mouth a little and Javier stuck the tablet in, then propped his head upright so he wouldn't choke. "Chew it. That's right." When Dale made a face, he knew they were on the right track. "Tastes awful, huh?"

"I hear sirens," Molly said. "Let me talk to him."

Javier stepped back and Molly leaned into the car, putting her arms around her uncle's neck and kissing his cheek. "We're going to get you help, Uncle Dale, I love you so much. Please, hang on. Trina and I need you."

He swallowed and lifted his head as if he were trying to speak.

"It's okay," she said, her voice soothing. "Just rest. The medics are almost here."

"Your aunt…" He was trying to say something, but even the effort made him clutch at his chest, restlessly.

"We'll take care of her too."

"But she…" He trailed off and leaned his head back. His eyes closed.

A tear ran down Molly's cheek as she stepped away. Behind them, an ambulance squealed to a stop.

The next few minutes were a blur of shouted instructions and questions as the medics eased Dale out onto a stretcher, cut away his shirt, and taped leads for an EKG.

"His wife's in the car, unconscious," Javier said.

"We think it's drugs." Molly's hands twisted together, over and over.

"Unrelated?" The second paramedic beckoned to the EMT who'd driven the ambulance and pointed toward the passenger side. The EMT, a young and nervous-looking redhead, jogged over to check on Lisa.

"She seems stable, but she's really out."

"We'll worry about him first."

Minutes later the tentative diagnosis came, just what Javier had guessed: heart attack.

The back door of Javier's car opened. "Mom? Mommy?"

Molly ran back and squatted beside Trina, their faces going red and pale with the flashing light.

Several of the neighbors came out, asking what they could do to help, and then Veronica pulled in behind Javier.

"Sir! Sir, how's the pain?" one of the medics barked out, and Dale shook his head.

"Blood ox's low," said the other.

"Let's get him in." The two male paramedics worked deftly, moving the large man into the ambulance. Immediately, one of the paramedics and the EMT set up oxygen while the other paramedic gave Lisa a more thorough look.

Javier approached Molly, Trina, and Veronica, who were in the middle of a conversation. "I want you to come home, Mom," Trina said. "But if you have to help Uncle Dale, it's okay. I can stay by myself."

"No way!" Veronica hugged the girl. "We're going to go back to your place and get you into bed. Unless you'd like a hot bath first."

They all looked at Trina. She was a tough cookie, but she'd been through a lot today. Javier wouldn't have been surprised if she'd burst into tears.

"I'm kind of hungry," Trina said.

Molly smiled, the tight lines of her face relaxing. "Stress always makes her hungry."

"Then we'll fix you some scrambled eggs with cheese. Even I can manage that."

"She burns toast," Javier said to Trina. "You might have to take charge of that part."

"Come on, kiddo." Veronica patted Trina's back. "Let's get out of here and fix some food. I'm hungry, too."

"I'll come home as soon as I can." Molly hugged Trina and then watched as she and Veronica walked away, arms around each other.

The paramedics were positioning Dale in the back of the ambulance.

"I'd like to ride along," Molly said to the paramedic in charge.

"Better not. We'll be busy and crowded in back."

"But—" She broke off, and the EMT put a hand on her shoulder. "He's going to make it. You can spend time with him in the hospital."

"Are you sure?" Her voice was as plaintive as a

little kid. But of course. Uncle Dale was a father figure to her, the kindest man in her life. To see him lying there with tubes and wires surrounding his inert body had to be awful for her.

Javier slipped an arm around her shoulders. "We'll follow the ambulance."

The paramedic in charge hurried over to Lisa, still sleeping in the passenger seat, and then looked at Javier. "Can you bring the lady? It'll be faster, but if you're not comfortable, we can call another ambulance for her."

"Sure can." Javier squeezed Molly's shoulders. "We'll go in Dale's car so we won't have to move Lisa. You can ride in back or drive your own car."

"I'll ride. Make sure she's okay."

On the short drive to the hospital, Lisa started tossing restlessly and mumbling. Molly spoke to soothe her, and Lisa sat bolt upright. "You took him away," she said. "He was mine and you took him away."

"What?" Javier barked, driving over the speed limit to keep pace with the ambulance. "Your husband's in the ambulance. They're just taking him to the hospital, not away from you."

"Petey. Why, Petey, of course!" Lisa mumbled something incoherent as they stopped for a traffic light while the ambulance flew on out of sight.

Molly's eyes widened. "Petey wasn't your husband, he was Mariana's."

"He was mine," Lisa said.

All of a sudden, Javier started to get the picture, and some of Lisa's motivations shifted into place. He was too tired to be tactful. "Were you having an affair with Petey?"

Molly gasped.

"He was going to leave that dishrag and marry me." Lisa's voice was stronger now, more certain.

A bolt of anger shot through Javier. "That's my cousin you're calling a dishrag. She was his wife. You should've respected that."

Lisa sat upright and grabbed his arm with surprising strength, causing the car to swerve.

He hit the brakes and shook her off, shoved her back into the passenger seat. "Put that seat upright and make sure she's buckled in," he told Molly as the car glided to a halt.

As Molly leaned over the front seat, fumbling for the seatbelt, Lisa grabbed her.

"Hey!" Molly's exclamation cut off abruptly. In its place came a choking noise.

"Get your hands off her!" Javier yanked Lisa's arms away by the wrists, not bothering to be gentle. "Are you okay?" he asked Molly.

"I'm..." She swallowed convulsively. "Yeah. I guess." She sank back into the backseat, her hands going to her throat.

"Let go of me!" Lisa screamed.

But when he did, she reached past him and jerked the car into drive again. It jolted forward and Javier spun back in his seat and slammed on the brakes, then turned off the car and pocketed the keys.

Lisa was beating at his arms and shoulders, screaming. She wasn't a large woman, but her strength suggested either mania or drugs. He got his arms around her from behind, effectively straightjacketing her.

Molly scrambled out, breathing hard. "I'm calling 9-1-1. Again."

Javier just sat, holding the thrashing, sobbing woman and trying not to think about all the ugliness he'd discovered that day and night. It was going to take a little time to process all of it.

Hours LATER, Molly collapsed into a chair at her kitchen table, gratefully accepting a cup of coffee from Veronica. The sky was growing lighter by the minute. It felt indescribably good to be in her own home with her daughter safely sleeping in the next room. Javier and Veronica were treating Molly like she was made of glass, and that was fine with her.

"So she got into her drug habit through Petey?" Veronica asked, pushing cream and sugar at Molly.

"Apparently so," Javier said. "That's part of what she was screaming as the police took her away."

Molly stirred cream and sugar into her coffee, focusing on the brown-and-white swirls. There would be time, later, to think about what had happened with Petey all those years ago. To reframe the reasons why Aunt Lisa had been so very, very angry about Petey's attentions to Molly, and why she hadn't wanted to believe Molly's story of the assault.

"What about Dale?" Veronica asked. "Is he going to be okay?"

"He's in good hands and he's stable. We won't be sure until tomorrow... well, today... how much damage there was to his heart." Molly reached out and took a hand of each of the Quintanas. "You two will never know how much your help has meant to me. I don't have much of a family, and..." Her throat tightened. "And you guys helped me save what's left of it, Trina and Dale."

"You can be a part of our family," Veronica said, standing up to hug her. After a minute, she straightened. "I mean that. But right now, I'm going home to get a couple of hours of sleep. Text me if you need me." She gently smacked her brother on the back. "And you. Take good care of her, you hear?"

After she'd left, Molly looked over at Javier to find him looking back at her. "How're you doing?" she asked.

"I'm beat," he admitted, "but I don't think I can sleep. You?"

"Same," she said.

"What should we do? Or... do you want to be alone? I can leave..."

She shook her head. "No. I want to talk to you." She didn't know what she was going to say, but there were issues to work out between her and this man, and she didn't want to wait another moment to do it. "Javier, I'm really sorry I didn't trust you enough to tell you the truth back when... when everything happened."

He reached across the tabletop and clasped her hand. "I understand. I wouldn't have told me, either. I can be way too judgmental."

"Still?" she asked.

"What do you mean?"

"Do you still judge me for it?"

"Oh, Molly." He came to kneel in front of her chair, taking both of her hands in his and looking up at her, so unbearably handsome that a lump came into her throat. "You suffered through a terrible assault, basically alone. Anyone would have understood if you'd decided on adoption for your baby. Some wouldn't have let Trina been born." A muscle twitched in his jaw. "But you, you brought Trina into this world and you cared for her alone. You've raised her up into a strong, courageous young lady who's going to set the world on fire."

Molly drew in a shaky breath. "As a parent, you

never know if you're doing it right. Believe me, there have been plenty of times—and today was one of them—when I've questioned everything I've done for Trina."

"Yet you carry on. Come here." He rose gracefully and tugged her over to the couch. He sat down close beside her and put an arm around her shoulders. "Is this okay?"

It was more than okay. It felt wonderful. But she didn't know what it meant. "I'm glad you admire me as a mother," she started. Then she went quiet. Because what was she going to say? That she felt more, much more, than friendship and admiration for him? She couldn't be the first to say it. Not with traditional, old-fashioned Javier.

"Molly," he said. "I admire a lot more about you than your mothering skills. You've become a successful professional and you're turning my family's restaurant around."

She stole a glance up at him. "Does that mean you're going to let me implement the rest of the changes, going forward?" she asked slyly.

He laughed down at her and pulled her closer. "It depends. If we're working together, are we allowed to fraternize?"

"Do you want to?"

For answer, he pulled her into a kiss that swept her into the past and the future, making her world explode.

Some time later, he stroked her cheek. "We have a lot to work out, Molly. I know you have challenges ahead. Dale, and Lisa, and—"

"And me!" Mariana was standing outside the screen door, knocking on the side of it. "What's going on in there?"

Molly sighed and stood. "Come in, Mariana. Would you like some coffee?"

"No, I want to know the story. First I hear that you caused my husband to cheat on me. Now, I hear that it was something else entirely."

Molly was exhausted and exhilarated and she couldn't imagine getting through this discussion. *Lord, help me remember this woman is hurting.*

"I never meant to cause you problems in your marriage," she said as she ushered Mariana to a seat across from the couch where Javier was sitting. Then she sat down beside him. "I was a child, and I didn't understand why he was... favoring me."

Mariana frowned.

"Did you ever know him to use or deal drugs?" Molly asked.

Mariana went pale and glanced at Javier.

"Did you?" he asked sharply.

Mariana nodded slowly. "I knew he was using. That was a big part of what took him so young."

"Did it go further than that, into selling?" Molly

crossed her arms over her stomach. She didn't look forward to telling Mariana the truth about her Aunt Lisa, but it had to come out. "Because I heard, recently, that he was both using and selling."

"Did Petey tend toward affairs?" Javier asked bluntly.

Mariana's eyes filled with tears. "I... There were some... indiscretions. He told me when he was dying. I always felt like it was my fault, like if I had been a better wife, pleased him more—"

"None of that," Javier said firmly. "Petey made a promise to you. If he didn't keep it, that wasn't your fault."

"But I loved him," Mariana said, crying openly. "In spite of everything, I loved him so much. I tried to be a good wife. And he still left me!"

Molly looked over at Javier and nodded toward Mariana, and he went to his cousin, sat on the side of her chair and put an arm around her. "Hey. This has brought up a lot for you. It wouldn't be a bad idea to talk to the pastor about it."

Mariana nodded, sniffling.

"In the meantime," Molly said, clearing her throat and trying to hold herself together, "we have three young girls who are going to be watching how we handle this. It's a very tough situation. What do you think we should do?"

Mariana studied her. "I'm sorry for what I said. I

talked more to Laura and Raquel about their conversation with Trina. She told them that Petey... that he forced himself on you. How can you handle seeing her every day?"

"That doesn't surprise you, that he did that?" Molly asked.

Mariana looked down at the floor, then raised her eyes to meet Molly's. "No. It doesn't."

"Were there others?" *Please, God, no.*

"Not that I know about. But he... he was harsh with me." She bit her lip, then put her hands to her face and leaned forward, sobbing.

Molly drew in a breath and let it flow back out. *What a world of hurt Petey had caused.*

"Why didn't you come to me?" Javier asked.

Mariana sat up, and she and Molly exchanged glances. "It's not that easy for a woman."

"*I* should have come forward," Molly said, "and I'll always regret that I didn't."

"Times were different when we were younger," Mariana said. "But we're raising girls who would never let that happen. Teaching them to be strong and independent and to fight for themselves." She looked at Molly. "At least I am. That's my revenge."

Molly nodded. "I feel the same."

"As for what the girls know and understand about it... It'll take some talking and praying. Maybe counseling. But when it's all said and done, I'd like for the girls to know Trina as a sister."

Molly swallowed hard. "I'd like that, too."

THREE WEEKS LATER, at the end of September, Javier drove toward El Corazon with some last-minute supplies for the final hour of the grand reopening. He'd volunteered to run out to Wernsman Farm because he'd needed time to himself. He felt reflective, grateful... but a little on edge.

In the end, everything had gone back to normal surprisingly fast.

Uncle Dale was home from the hospital and recovering well. A visiting nurse kept tabs on him, and Molly stopped in every day. They both seemed to be treasuring their relationship even more after the challenges and threats to it.

Lisa was in rehab, and the drugs they'd found on her person at the hospital meant that charges had been filed against her. When she got out, she'd stand trial.

As soon as he was strong enough, Dale insisted he was going to divorce her and start his life over again. Molly, surprisingly, was advocating for them to try marriage counseling, but so far, Dale was adamant.

Terrance McKinley had been brought before a judge for what he'd done to Trina, and given a stark choice: a military school, or juvie. He'd chosen the former and was already gone from town.

As he got closer to the restaurant, Javier could hear

the band and see the twinkle lights. The late-September weather had cooperated by giving them a warm day, and they'd rented heaters for the evening so they could keep the outdoor seating area open.

Hmmm, maybe they should consider adding a permanent outdoor area, or a porch that could be open or closed. People sure seemed to be having fun. Hiring a small Mexican pop band had been a good decision, apparently, because both older and younger people were dancing.

Javier got out of the car with his bags of fresh cilantro, tomatoes, and tomatillos, gratified to see how many cars were already in the parking lot. It would take time to rebuild the restaurant's reputation, but he could already see the difference. The food tasted better, and the new wait staff—girls, no less—were courteous and enthusiastic, as well-mannered as his mother would have wished. Maria was reveling in the opportunity to cook more authentic, natural foods, and Pablo, though cautious, seemed happier on the job, now that they'd hired another cook so he wasn't so overworked.

El Corazon could be an asset to the community and a centerpiece of town again, just as his parents had wanted. Not the same, not exactly, but right for the times.

He walked into the kitchen and the woman who was responsible for so many of the changes smiled a little shyly as she reached out to take the bags. "Thanks for getting that. I don't know how we miscalculated what we'd need for today."

Maria looked their way, her face flushed with the heat of the stove. "We miscalculated because the lines have been out the door all day. I never thought we'd get this big of a crowd."

"It was partly your abuela," Pablo said from where he stood, spooning *posole* into soup cups. It was one of the freebies they were offering with every meal today. "She spread the word among everyone she knows—"

"Which is everyone in town," Veronica added from the doorway.

"*And* she told them to tell the young people in their families about the new, fresh options and the more authentic heritage dishes," Maria chimed in. "My mama did the same thing with all her friends from the cancer support group. A lot of them are here with their families."

"Prayer group ladies, too," Veronica said.

Javier looked over at Molly. She was washing the tomatoes he'd just brought in, but a smile tickled the corner of her mouth.

He wanted to kiss that smile, but he hesitated. For one thing, it wasn't the time or place. For another, he wasn't sure how Molly felt about him. They'd spent time together in the past couple of weeks, but it had been a lot of talking things through or solving problems. Yeah, they'd kissed a couple of times, but she'd pulled away quickly.

"You were right," he told her, then turned to the rest of the kitchen staff. "You were all right, and I was wrong, okay?"

"Whoa, did I hear that right?" His brother Daniel held the door for his two little girls and then, with a father's practiced move, grabbed them by the shoulders before they could run into the main part of the kitchen. "That's one for the record books, Javier admitting he was wrong." He squatted down and put an arm around each twin. "We're just back here to say hello, okay? And sit a minute with Abuela and her friends. Then we're going to get some food for dinner and go back home."

"It's the grand opening," Veronica protested. "Don't you want to stick around a little while?"

"No. Because Mrs. Simpson is threatening to quit as the girls' after school child care provider, and I have to make phone calls and find backup."

"On a Saturday night?" Javier said.

"Trina and I can help out, if you need," Molly added.

"Thanks. Not necessary. Come on, girls, let's go visit with Abuela. Veronica, could you…"

"Of course, I'll make up a couple of boxes for you," she said. "Don't be offended, Molly. Daniel doesn't accept help from anyone."

Exhibit A, he was pulling money out of his wallet right now to pay for his and the girls' meal, even though he was a quarter owner in the restaurant.

Javier intercepted Molly on her way to the cutting boards. "That was nice of you," he said in a low voice. "Can we spend some time together once this is over?"

She bit her lip. "I have to see what Trina's up to."

"Trina's welcome to join us." Although, truthfully, he hoped she wouldn't. What he had to say to Molly was better kept between the two of them, at least for now.

"Mom!" Trina came into the restaurant, flushed and breathing hard.

"Were you dancing, sweetie?"

"Yeah! It's fun. And some of the kids are going to The Jukebox afterward for ice cream. Can I go?"

As Molly questioned Trina about the details and then ultimately gave her permission, Javier spoke to Veronica and slipped away. He had plans to make.

TWO HOURS LATER, Molly came out onto the porch of her cottage, wondering what Javier was up to. A shower and comfortable, casual clothes had revitalized her, but she still felt a little guilty about leaving everyone else with the cleanup at El Corazon.

The great news was, it had been a huge success.

They would continue to tweak the details going forward, but the basic changes were in place. Most importantly, everyone was on board with them. Even Javier.

Javier. In the past couple of weeks he'd been attentive, but circumspect. He had brought pizza from Fire and Brimstone one night, and had invited her and Trina to join a church group on a hike. When they'd encountered each other at the Cottages or El Corazon, they'd talked in a friendly way. And they'd had a couple of serious conversations about the past. But he hadn't made any kind of declaration of his feelings for her, and she felt on edge about that.

Now that he knew all that had happened to her, he wasn't angry. But aside from some long, searching glances, he'd been acting more like a friend than someone interested in a relationship.

That was fine, she informed her hungry heart. She had plenty to keep her busy. She was calling on potential clients and building her online business, now that El Corazon's needs were mostly being handled by the family. She was helping Trina manage the fact that she'd become a minor celebrity at middle school after her heroic attack had gotten rid of Terrance, a longtime bully who'd been bothering younger kids for years.

There was no need to focus on Javier and what he felt or didn't feel for her. Still, her heart wouldn't slow down, wondering what he had planned for them. He'd acted… different, when he'd asked her to get together tonight.

He pulled up in a car that looked a whole lot fancier than the one he usually drove. Suddenly, she felt underdressed.

But when he got out and trotted up the stairs, she saw that he was wearing jeans, too. "Are you ready?" he asked, giving her a killer smile. "You look beautiful."

She glanced down at her casual red shirt and jeans. If he thought *this* outfit was beautiful, maybe he did have special feelings for her. "Where are we going?"

"You'll see." He escorted her to the passenger side and opened the door, and she slid into luxurious leather comfort. "Don't get too excited," he said. "It's Alex's car. I'm just borrowing it."

Why had he borrowed Alex's car? He'd been content with his own vehicle up until now.

They drove for just a few minutes, ending up at Arcadia Creek Park. When they pulled in, Molly thought she caught a glimpse of Trina walking through the picnic area, but when Javier came around and opened her car door and she got out, there was nobody there.

"Was that Trina, or was I seeing things? She's supposed to be at The Jukebox."

"I didn't see her," Javier said blandly. "Do you

want to text her?"

She did, and quickly, a text came back. "Jukebox is a great place! Having fun."

So that was good. She took the elbow Javier offered her and they turned toward the picnic area. And gasped.

Candles in hurricane glasses lined the swinging bridge and made a path to the scattered picnic tables.

Javier intertwined his fingers with hers. "Come on, let's follow the lights."

Her breath caught. Was he planning something special or were there always lights here?

"Don't worry," he said, obviously misinterpreting her confusion. "There's very little fire danger with this kind of holder, and anyway, someone will blow them out soon."

Typical Javier, being a worrywart. No one would get into danger, ever, on his watch.

He led her along, over the swinging bridge and along the lamplit path to a picnic table set with chocolate and a tiny bottle of champagne.

Molly's heart started pounding impossibly hard. Why would a man set such a romantic scene, unless—

"I wanted to thank you for what you did," Javier said.

Molly's heart sank. This was a thank you? *Just* a thank you? Her face flamed hot because she'd hoped—for an instant—that it was more.

Javier tugged her to the table. "I need to talk to you."

"Okay." Her voice sounded breathless to her own ears.

"Let's sit down." He guided her to a seat in the middle of the table, facing the lighted bridge.

Her stomach somersaulted. No matter how hard she tried to tell herself to calm down, this felt momentous.

"Molly, how do you feel about what's been happening between us the past couple of weeks?"

"Ummm... it's been fun?"

His face fell. "Is that all?"

"No," she said softly, looking away. "It's been a lot more but..."

He touched her chin. "But what?"

"But I'm afraid to hope," she said, and then clamped her mouth shut. She didn't dare say more, reveal more of her feelings, until she knew what was on his mind.

"It's been more to me, too," he said, and got down on one knee, taking both of her hands in his.

"Javier! Stop!" If this was some kind of joke... "What are you doing?"

He reached out to cup her face in his two hands. "I'm trying to tell you," he said, "that I love you and I want to marry you."

She gasped and the butterflies in her stomach took

wing. "Did I... " She cocked her head to one side. Had she heard him right? Wonderful things like this didn't happen to unloved orphan girls who'd gotten pregnant without being married.

Except she knew now that Petey's assault hadn't been her fault. She *wasn't* the terrible person she'd thought she was. God hadn't caused it, but he had worked it for good.

Javier peered into her eyes as if trying to read her thoughts. "We loved each other once. Misunderstandings and horrible life events split us apart, but that initial love and caring never went away, at least on my side. Did it on yours?"

She shook her head. "Come sit beside me. I feel funny with you down there."

"You didn't answer," he said as he rose to sit on the bench next to her, putting an arm loosely around her shoulders as if afraid to pull her closer. "Do you still have any of the feelings toward me that you used to have?"

When she glanced over at his face, she saw that it was creased with concern and worry. That was Javier: confident on the outside, but just a little insecure on the inside. She leaned into him. "I still have all those feelings and more."

His arm tightened around her shoulders, the warmth of it making her feel protected and safe. "We talked marriage thirteen years ago and it made sense," he said. "For me, it still makes sense. Will you consider it?"

She nodded, staring down at her knees, suddenly shy.

"How much time do you need? I'm not... well, I *am* in a rush, but for you, I can wait."

"We don't have to wait," she whispered.

"What did you say?"

She turned to face him. "I would like nothing better than to marry you," she said, "and the sooner, the better."

Joy spread across his face, and his eyes went shiny. "Oh, Molly. You've just made me very, very happy." He pulled her to him in a tender kiss.

Suddenly applause rang out. Cries of "that's so romantic" and "I *knew* they liked each other" burst out through the picnic area as lamps lit all over.

Molly pulled away and sat upright, feeling jarred that their private moment had been hijacked. But then she looked around, and her hand flew to her mouth.

At every picnic table was someone she cared about. Trina and her friends; Mariana, Laura, and Raquel; Veronica, Alex, and Patricia; Maria and the prayer group. Even Uncle Dale, in a wheelchair with his visiting nurse beside him. No one was close enough to hear what they'd been saying, but they must have seen the embrace and kiss.

She stared at Javier. "You were sure of success!"

"No! No, it was the opposite. I wanted support to force me to go through with it. I figured... either way, you'd like to have your friends around you."

"And he had to ask *me*, first," Trina cried as she ran to them, flopped down beside Molly, and hugged her hard. "I thought about it, and I decided I'd like him for a stepdad. If that's okay with you."

"Of course, I said yes, but... when did you talk to Trina?" she asked, looking from Javier to her daughter and back again.

"Two days ago! It's been so hard not to spill the secret."

Molly's mouth dropped open, but before she could speak, the prayer group came over. "We've been praying for you," Maria said, "and when Javier said he wanted us to be nearby when he proposed, well..."

"We decided it was probably meant to be," Charlotte said. "We've been over there praying for an hour."

Tears filled Molly's eyes as looked around at all her friends. "I... I don't know what to say."

"I just know it's going to make our families even more connected." Raquel pulled Trina up and into a hug, and Laura immediately joined in.

"It's true," Mariana said to Molly. "You'll be my cousin's wife, and so Trina will be..." She trailed off, frowning.

"Our cousin *and* our sister!" Laura burst out,

keeping an arm around Trina. "We're going to have so much fun!"

Gratitude washed over Molly. She squeezed Javier's hand and smiled at Trina. "I guess we're staying in Arcadia Valley."

"Can we, Mom, for real and for always?"

"Well," she said, glancing over at Javier. "We never know what adventures lie ahead or what the Lord has in mind. But for now and the foreseeable future... yes, we're staying in Arcadia Valley."

Cheers and applause broke out around them.

Suddenly, romantic music came from the dark. "Sorry, I only now remembered," came Veronica's voice. She hurried over to them. "I was supposed to be playing music this whole time."

"I didn't even think of it," Javier said. "I was only thinking of Molly and whether she was going to say yes or no."

Molly leaned back on his shoulder and looked up into his eyes. "You should have known I'd say yes."

He shook his head. "I take nothing for granted."

"Do you like the ring, Mom?" Trina asked.

"The ring!" Javier clapped a hand to his forehead. He stood, reached into his pocket, and went back down on one knee. "Could you hold out your hand?" he asked Molly.

What woman would ever say no to that? She extended her hand, and he slid the most exquisite, vintage-style ring, a round-cut diamond surrounded by a halo of smaller diamonds.

Molly's eyes widened as she stared from the ring to his face. "It's exactly what I would have chosen," she said, tears filling her eyes again. "How did you know?"

"Because *I* showed him your jewelry box," Trina said. "I even let him borrow your turquoise ring so he could get the right size."

Molly's heart warmed. Even more than she loved the ring, she loved the fact that Javier had involved Trina in the preparation and decision-making.

"Would you like to dance," he whispered in her ear, "or is that too corny?"

She laughed at him. "Have you gotten better since high school? I'm kind of fond of my toes."

"I've worked on it." He pulled her up as Veronica jogged over and changed the song. As "Fly Me to the Moon" started to play, Javier pulled her into a foxtrot that had nothing to do with the awkward way they'd danced in high school. She felt his strong arms around her, leaned her head against his broad chest.

He would protect and care for her and Trina, yes, but he also respected her as a woman. "I'm so happy right now," she whispered up to him.

"You've made me the happiest man alive."

Javier waved a hand behind her back, and she glanced around to see that Trina and most of the others were dancing, too. Even Uncle Dale rocked back and forth in his wheelchair, snapping his fingers. As Molly watched, Beatriz approached him and gently spun him around.

Gratitude filling her heart, Molly looked skyward. Her heavenly father had brought her back to Arcadia Valley for a lot of reasons, but this was the prize one. She would spend the rest of her life with the man she loved, living in a community of friends and family, doing her work. Her heart almost bursting, she closed her eyes. *Thank you, Lord. I don't deserve this but I'm so, so grateful.*

"What are you thinking?" Javier asked, his breath warm against her ear.

Molly turned to him. "That I want you to kiss me."

And he did.

# Arcadia Valley Romance
## Six authors. Six series. One community.

Welcome to Arcadia Valley, Idaho, where a foodie culture and romance grow hand-in-hand. Join my friends and me as we release a book every month set in Arcadia Valley. You'll enjoy meeting old friends and making new ones as each of the six authors' books intertwine with the previous stories in this Christian romance series. Get started with *Romance Grows in Arcadia Valley* and follow along at ArcadiaValleyRomance.com to make sure you don't miss any installments!

AN

*Arcadia Valley*

ROMANCE

www.ArcadiaValleyRomance.com

# Next in the Arcadia Valley Romance Series

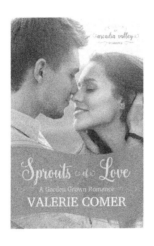

## Can love sprout amid a tsunami of vegetables?

Single mom Evelyn Felton takes on a third part-time job managing a greenhouse and garden project for Grace Fellowship. Formerly homeless, she's thrilled to offer truckloads of fresh produce to the Arcadia Valley food bank.

If only Ben Kujak weren't running Corinna's Cupboard singlehandedly, he'd be delighted to be on the receiving end. But Evelyn and her dynamo daughter, Maisie, won't take no for an answer, even if it means restructuring Ben's charity.

Soon Ben finds himself wishing they'd transform his personal life, too, but can true love sprout when their pasts collide with the present?

# Chapter 1,
## Sprouts of Love by Valerie Comer

YOU'RE EVELYN FELTON?"

Um, yes. Last she'd checked. The man filling the entrance to Corinna's Cupboard couldn't be a minute over twenty-five, but that didn't stop him from acting like he owned the place. Eyebrows raised, he appraised her from steely blue eyes.

What had she ever done to him? Nothing. She'd never seen him before... had she? Evelyn stiffened her back and kept the smile in place. "Yes, I'm Evelyn, and I'm here to meet with Ben Kujak about donating garden-grown produce. Is he in?"

Silence reigned for several heartbeats.

Had she asked such a difficult question? The building this charity operated just north of Arcadia Valley's Main Street wasn't that big. If Mr. Kujak wasn't stocking shelves or applying for grants, he likely wasn't on the premises.

The upstart chewed his lip then nodded, stepping aside. "With a name like Evelyn, I was expecting someone older."

He had to be kidding. Her name wasn't Matilda or Ethel. Evelyn tightened her grip on her messenger bag and raised her eyebrows. "I'm not sure what that's supposed to mean. You haven't answered my question. Is Mr. Kujak available? If not, when's a good time to meet him?"

Muscles rippled the length of his arm as he stretched out his hand. "I'm Ben. Come on in."

"I, um..." She blinked and shook his hand briskly. "Hi." Nobody had told her the man who'd worked miracles starting a charity from nothing was little more than a kid. Scratch that. Definitely not a child, not with how attractive he looked in those cargo shorts and gray T-shirt. Not with his light-brown hair matching the stubble that graced his cheeks and chin.

Evelyn shook her head and took a deep breath. "Like you, I thought I was meeting with someone older."

She'd counted on it, actually. Not that she was easily distracted by good-looking men close to her age, but there was something secure about working with someone older. Somebody who was a husband, a father, maybe even a grandfather. Someone who could guide her as she took on the management of her daughter's ingenious project of using the Akers Garden Center's former greenhouses to grow food for the needy.

Evelyn had no idea what she was doing. She'd

truly hoped the recipient of their hard work could smooth the transition. Instead, she was stuck with Mr. Do-Good, Junior.

Ben's face morphed into a half-smile. "Well, now that we've gotten all that out of the way, come on into my office." He led the way through a space with tall, sturdy shelving containing a smattering of canned and packaged goods.

How many times had she clutched little Maisie by the hand and searched for something besides boxed macaroni and cheese and over-sweetened cereals on shelves like these? Clouds of uncertainty and desperation had permeated their entire life back in Memphis. They hadn't completely dissipated even with Idaho's fresh air and blue summer sky.

Evelyn followed him past another storage room and into a small office. She stopped in the doorway as though she'd rammed into a glass wall. Bricks shored up one corner of a chipped pressboard desk. It was impossible to discern what type of wood it was pretending to be between all of the folders and papers in awkward stacks, threatening to slide. Her gaze followed the likely avalanche path to the concrete floor where a few papers and a Styrofoam cup lay beside a full trash can.

Her fingers itched to toss the cup, haul out the garbage, and file this man's papers. How could he get a stitch of work done in a disaster like this?

Ben pointed at an orange plastic chair. "Have a seat." He rounded the desk, scooped together the loose papers in the work area, and deposited them on top of the tallest stack of folders before pulling out his own chair. "Now, what exactly do you want from me?"

*Ask not what your food pantry can do for you...*

Evelyn perched on the edge of the orange chair and clutched her messenger bag to her chest. "I'm not sure where to start." Why couldn't she remember the speech she'd rehearsed?

He glanced at the clock above the window.

Man, he didn't need to be rude. She took a deep breath. "I'm not sure if you're aware, but elderly Mr. Akers set up a living trust in conjunction with Grace Fellowship. The property in question used to belong to Akers Garden Center and contains an old house, two greenhouses, and numerous garden beds. Volunteers have been growing vegetables there since June, and the first pickings of peas and greens will be ready to harvest in about a week."

"I'm sorry, but I'm not certain what this has to do with me." Ben leaned back in his chair.

Evelyn flinched as it creaked.

Hadn't she just told him? "The volunteers are growing produce for Corinna's Cupboard. We understand that you feed hot meals three evenings a week, and we think that's fantastic. We want to help supply ingredients. It's all yours."

"Uh... that's great. What format exactly are these vegetables coming in?"

She beamed at him brightly. "Garden fresh." He could smile and say thanks anytime.

The man closed his eyes and pinched the bridge of his nose.

Evelyn frowned. "They're organic. Fresh. Full of flavor and nutrients." Why did she feel she had to sell the guy on garden-grown veggies? Didn't he care about the needs of the people for whom he supplied food? Didn't he realize how much money this would save the charity?

Ben took a deep breath and looked across the disastrous desk at her. "Look, Ms. Felton, that sounds wonderful."

She beamed.

"But I'm one man. I don't have time to prepare meals for forty people from scratch. I have a basic menu I rotate through every two weeks, and that's all I can do."

One man? One guy did this all by himself? "I-I don't understand."

"There's nothing to understand. I'm not a superhero. I'm one normal guy who happens to run this place single-handedly, and I don't have time to cook from raw ingredients. Thanks for thinking of Corinna's Cupboard, but you'll need to find another outlet for your vegetables." Ben rose. "Was there anything else? Because I have something I need to be doing."

Like cleaning his office? Evelyn stood. "But..."

"I'm sorry, Evelyn. I really am." He gestured toward the door. "I'd need to be at least three people to handle what you're offering, and I'm not."

IF BEN COULDN'T stop thinking about that meeting with Evelyn Felton out of his mind, he'd never get anything done. What a contrast she'd been to the needy people who frequented Corinna's Cupboard. She was so vibrant. So full of confidence. So pretty.

So much like Corinna had been.

About that. Extra work aside, he didn't need to notice a woman. He liked donors who sent checks in the mail, hit the donate button on the charity's website, or contributed to one of the many fundraisers his former in-laws held across the country. Also acceptable: having cases of canned or packaged goods delivered by the local freight company. Meeting donors face to face only took time he couldn't afford out of his schedule.

Ben drove his hands through his hair. Enough with Evelyn. What had he been doing when she arrived? Counting size-10 cans of peas on the shelf. Hadn't been that hard to count all the way to two.

He and Corinna had bought that acreage with the

creek running through it shortly after their wedding with help from her parents. She'd put in a garden amidst the volcanic outcroppings on the property. They'd sat on the back porch, shelling peas into a large bowl and eating them just as quickly, popping the rounded end and sliding their thumbs down the interior of the pod, dislodging the little green orbs. Happy memories of a happier time.

He glared at the huge cans of peas on the shelf. They hailed from a different planet, but he'd told Evelyn the truth. He didn't have time for that much food prep.

All of the shelves were rather bare, but that wasn't unusual. God always provided what Ben needed when he needed it.

Was God trying to provide him with fresh peas? Sweet, succulent peas?

He snorted a laugh as he made his way back to the dismal office. God had better supply an army of volunteers while He was at it.

Ben stopped in the doorway. What had Evelyn seen? His stomach curdled. A full-on disaster. How had it gotten this way? The fourth-hand file cabinet had given up and all but collapsed. He'd removed the files and dumped them on any flat surface. The cabinet was unsalvageable, but he hadn't yet bothered to haul it to the curb on trash day.

He'd gotten in such a rut. Why not just go buy a

new file cabinet? He might not want to ask his in-laws for money for that, but he could buy it himself. He could forego riding Halim this afternoon and drive into Twin Falls. It wasn't a hot meal day, and the regulars had already come in to pick up day-old bread. He could lock up early.

If Corinna could see him now—see the food cupboard that bore her name—what would she think? Would she be glad he was making a difference, or would she chastise him for the mess it was all in?

He could see the glimmer in Evelyn's narrowed eyes when she looked at his towering paperwork, and he'd spent under fifteen minutes in her presence.

A file cabinet. It was a good place to start. He strode toward the door, fingering the keys in his shorts' pocket.

What if... what if there was something to Evelyn's offer?

Her brown hair, artfully messy, had flowed halfway down her back. Corinna's had been shorter. Black. Evelyn's eyes flashed amber in her eagerness then faded to brown when he'd squashed her hopes. He'd teased Corinna that gazing into her eyes was like drowning in pure coffee.

Why was he even comparing the two women? Corinna was gone, and Evelyn wasn't offering herself as a replacement. No. She offered vegetables. He needed vegetables. Ben's mouth watered. He really liked them fresh from the garden, personally.

He locked up the building. It was just as ugly as the others on this block. Red brick like most of the older storefronts, scuffed and watermarked with age, it crowded the chipped sidewalk. Main Street had been revitalized in the past few years, pulling residents back to shopping locally. A block behind Main? Still stuck a hundred years in the past, Corinna's Cupboard shared a block with a tattoo parlor, a couple of bars, a thrift store, and several boarded-up buildings.

Without making a conscious choice, he drove the few blocks out of his way to pass the old Akers' greenhouses. His eyes widened as he rounded the end of the block and saw a row of garden beds overflowing with lush greenery. All that had grown in the six weeks since the beginning of June?

The truck coasted to a stop at the curb. Ben slid out and walked around to stand on the sidewalk.

Several people worked among the beds. Looked like folks were staking and pruning tomatoes. A kid of about ten knelt by the bed nearest him, plucking tufts of green. She glanced over at him.

"Hi." Ben lifted a hand in greeting, his gaze shifting back to the amazing lush scene in front of him. This was what Evelyn had been talking about? Wow.

"Want to help?" the girl asked. "There's lots to do."

Ben turned back to her. What would happen if he

played dumb? "I haven't been down this street for a while. What's going on?"

The girl stood and stripped off the dirt-smeared gloves she'd been wearing. Her dark blond hair stuck out of the ponytail trying to corral it. "This here is a project from that church over there." She thumbed toward the brick building housing Grace Fellowship a couple of blocks closer to downtown. "The old man wrote a living... a living something. He wanted us to use this place for something that would help people."

Ben searched his earlier conversation for the right words. "Living trust?"

She snapped her fingers. "That's it. I'm Maisie. Who're you? Want to sign up? Cameron's over there. He can help you."

"I'm, uh, Ben." His name wouldn't mean anything to her. "I'm kind of busy these days, so I probably won't volunteer for anything. Thanks, though."

Maisie shoved her hands into the pockets of her shorts. "Everyone's busy." She tilted her head to look up at him. "Did you know that there's lots of people in Arcadia Valley who don't have enough food? Maybe even hundreds."

Why did a kid her age know that or even care? *Play along, Ben.* "Really? Right here?"

"Some of them don't have jobs. And some of them are drunks." She pursed her lips. "There's all kinds of reasons."

"I've noticed a man sitting on the sidewalk holding out a hat."

"That's probably Hiram. The doctors had to cut off his leg because of diabetes and he couldn't work anymore."

Ben narrowed his gaze at this child who was barely taller than his waist. "Yes, that's him. Do you know him?"

"I talk to him sometimes. But I usually don't have anything to give him because the old woman by the park is always hungry. I feel bad if I don't give her half my sandwich."

"Rona?" the name slipped out before Grady could censure it.

Maisie tipped her head at him and gave him a closer look. "Yeah. Rona. You know her? Nobody knows her."

Was he going to tell this child who he was? That he worked to better the lives of people like Hiram and Rona? People most others ignored or jeered? He opened his mouth to confess all but, for some reason, reluctance halted his words.

No, he had too much to think about to get embroiled in whatever this kid knew. Whatever this project was for. If they wanted to give him fresh food, couldn't they have thought of the fact they should give him volunteers as well?

Maisie had asked him to join the work here. He bit

back a sardonic laugh. He should ask her to volunteer for him... but he wouldn't, because she might agree. Might show him up. But, a soup kitchen was no place for a kid.

Ben nodded sagely and offered a smile. "Thanks for telling me about them. It's nice to find people who care." He turned toward his truck. "Have a great evening."

"If you care about them, you should help us grow food for them."

Ben clamped down on his jaw and didn't turn back. Little did she know.

Want more? Order the book here!

arcadiavalleyromance.com/books/sprouts-of-love